Sportswriter

William Baer

Southwell Press

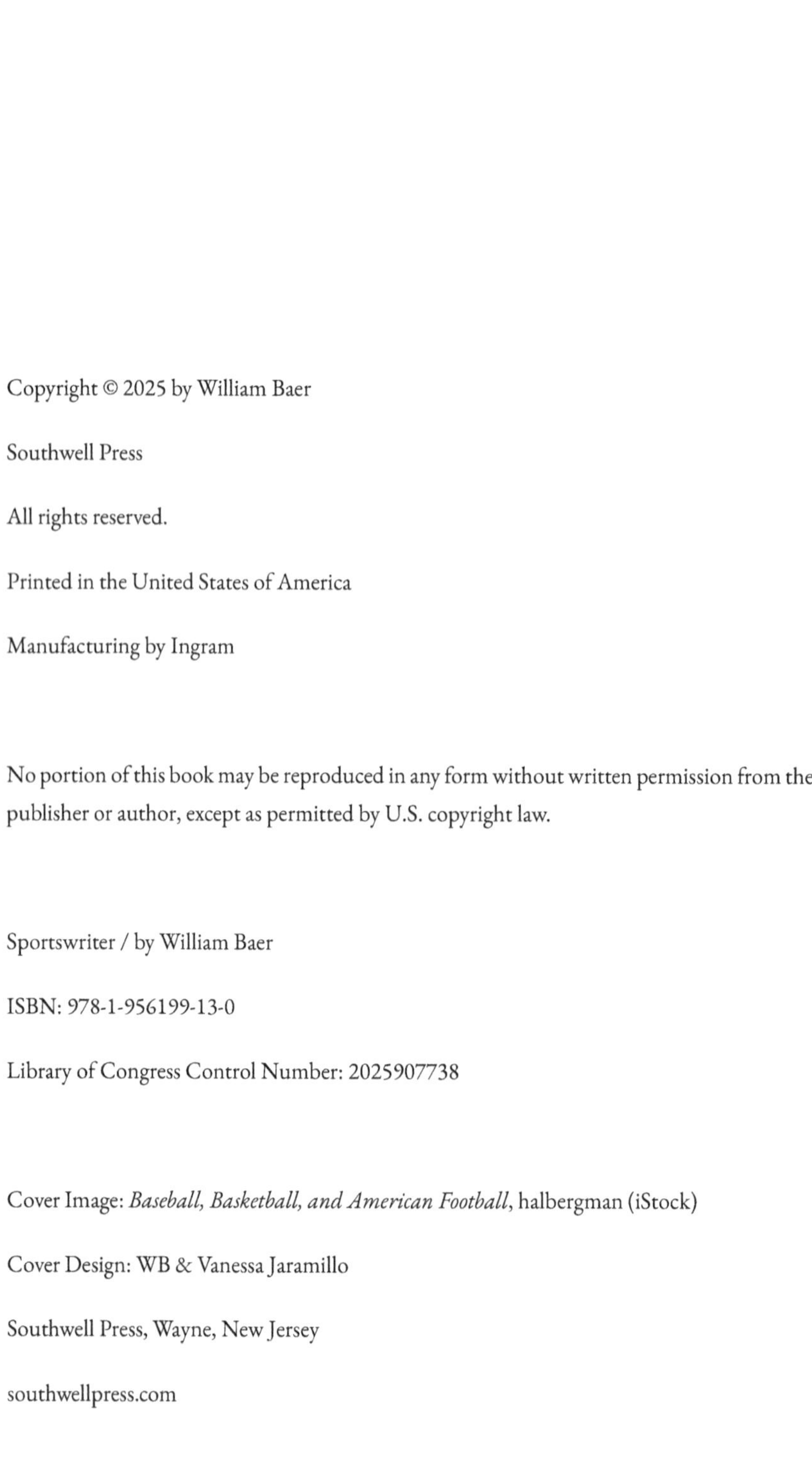

Sportswriter / by William Baer

ISBN: 978-1-956199-13-0

Library of Congress Control Number: 2025907738

Cover Image: *Baseball, Basketball, and American Football*, halbergman (iStock)

Cover Design: WB & Vanessa Jaramillo

Southwell Press, Wayne, New Jersey

southwellpress.com

for my family and friends

"All personal crises are spiritual crises."
– Fr. John Colt

I.

2021

Chapter 1

Madison Square Garden

(Saturday, 12/11/21)

Unanimous decision.

Lopsided as hell.

In the seventh round, Loma dropped Commey with a left hook which put the former IBF lightweight champ on queer street. It was so bad that Lomachenko was actually pleading with Commey's corner to throw in the towel before their fighter got seriously hurt. They didn't listen. Courageously, Commey managed to survive the rest of the fight as Loma picked up the WBO lightweight title to add to his long list of impressive accomplishments, as he moved forward on his way to the Hall of Fame.

Yes, the Russian/Putin bastards have been threatening his homeland, but the Ukrainian fighter still seemed focused and undistracted, and he fought like a warrior.

Let's face it, there's nothing like a fight at the Garden, the greatest sports venue in the entire world. There's also nothing like a championship fight. Joyce Carol Oates once wrote in her excellent *On Boxing*:

> *The delirium of the crowd at one of those matches called "great" must be experienced first-hand to be believed (Frazier-Ali I, 1971, Hagler-Hearns, 1986, for instance).*

Tonight's fight was hardly in a class with those two legendary fights, but it was still an exciting championship fight at Madison Square Garden. When my old man was a nineteen-year-old kid, he'd attended the Frazier-Ali "Fight of the Century" right here at the Garden. As for me, I've been covering sports (mostly baseball and boxing) for almost fifteen years and the closest I've ever gotten to one of those rare super-fights was Arturo Gatti's extremely close decision in his first brawl with Micky Ward down in Atlantic City. I was seventeen at the time, and I was blown away by the clash that was eventually recognized as *Ring Magazine*'s Fight of the Year in 2003.

Tonight I'd come to the Garden alone, waving to some of the other reporters and ex-fighters and speaking briefly to a few others. Mostly at the fights I prefer to sit alone so I can focus, even on a night like tonight when I wasn't covering the fight for *SI* or the *Star-Ledger*. I'd come to the Garden tonight to simply watch and enjoy Lomachenko, a kid I've always liked ever since his consecutive Olympic golds at Beijing (2008) and London (2012).

After the decision, I decided not to go to his locker room or wait around for the post-fight presser, and I left the arena with the rest of the still-wired crowd.

Earlier tonight I'd had a rather disappointing dinner at Jack Doyle's with Zabrina Foster who had nothing else on her mind than ranting about sports inequities, so I was fine with just heading back home to New Jersey. I exited the Garden's main entrance on Seventh Avenue to try and hail a cab. As I walked over to the edge of the curb, I saw it coming.

Right at me.

A black van!

High speed!

Careening out of control.

There was no time to do anything except realize in a momentary flash that I was surely as good as dead.

Then at the very last instant, the van veered slightly to my right, brushed against my right side and knocked me down to the sidewalk, as the van immediately smashed into one of those huge stone planters outside the front of the Garden. There was a terrible crash, some panic in the crowd, and more than a few screams.

I rose to my feet slowly and looked around.

The van hadn't hit me directly. It felt more like a light thump against my right side which had knocked me off balance. I seemed to be OK. No one else on the sidewalk seemed to be hurt either, but the van was badly crushed and destroyed. It seemed unlikely that anyone inside would have survived. Stupidly, a bit brain numb, I walked over to the van, but I couldn't see very much. There was a lot of red blood mixed in with the shattered glass. Inside, there was just the driver.

A kid.

Soon the cops were all over the scene, setting up tape, moving the crowd back, and talking to me. Then the EMTs were on the scene. Then the jaws of life.

The kid had nearly killed me, but I seemed to be all right, so I got concerned about the kid. Silently, I asked St. Margaret to help him out.

As I stood around watching, I texted Katie. Then I called her. Naturally, I wanted her to come and get me, but she didn't respond and she didn't pick up, which irritated the hell out of me.

Where *was* she?

Katie *always* picks up.

Eventually, my phone vibrated.

Finally!

It was a text:

> *Meu Amor – I'll be in New York next week before return-ing to Caracas. Can we meet again? Love, Inês*

What?

What the hell was that?

It gave me the creeps.

Needless to say, I knew no one named Inês from Caracas or any-where else, and I had the feeling that the message was meant for my old man. My dead old man, who was Richard Ramsey Sr. to my Richard Ramsey Jr.

Maybe it was something ugly from his past.

I texted right back:

Who are you?

Then I hailed a cab.

Chapter 2

Copacabana

(Saturday, 12/11/21)

"What happened to you?" she asked with a smile.

I was sitting downstairs at the Copa with two enthusiastic boxing fans from Philadelphia. Adriana and Valentina. Both of whom were wearing Bernard Hopkins "Executioner" shirts. Both of whom were around my age, mid-thirties. Both of whom were better than good-looking, obviously full of Philly mischief, both knocking off piña coladas with alacrity.

Which is maybe why Adriana would ask the kind of thing you're not supposed to ask people.

She was curious about my eye patch.

I told them the truth.

"Baseball. A hard line drive."

That was all she needed.

"Good. I like it."

A lot of women feel that way.

My mom once told me that most women like a wounded male. But not *too* wounded.

"So behave yourself, Richie."

Which I can't say that I've done over the subsequent years.

After nearly getting run down and killed earlier, I really didn't feel like heading back to New Jersey. Katie still wasn't answering, and I thought to myself, "Screw her!" and decided to distract myself in the city. I took a cab up to 51st Street and went inside the Copa. Upstairs, I ran into my two Philly girls who were just coming off the packed and raucous dance floor. They'd been doing some kind of not-unappealing Philly Salsa to a cover of Celia Cruz's *"Cucala."* When Valentina bumped into me, she said something to her pal about the "handsome pirate" (I get a lot of that "pirate" business, but not so much of the "handsome" bit, neither of which I minded at all), and they both giggled about it. The pirate, by the way, was wearing a Hugo Boss dark navy suit.

Soon the three of us were heading downstairs to take an extended booze break at a corner table not too far from the DJ, who clearly liked Marc Anthony and La India.

Which was fine with me.

We swapped a lot of typical questions, found out that we were all at the Loma fight, and when I said my name, Adriana recognized it.

"Didn't you write a boxing book?"

"I did. Some baseball too."

They had no interest in hardball.

Adriana was referring to my *Fight of the Century*, which was published a few years ago in 2012.

"I loved that book!"

"Me too!" Valentina remembered, "Smokin' Joe smoked the Loudmouth."

It's true.

That legendary night at the Garden their Philly boy Joe had soundly battered Muhammad Ali in the most famous bout in boxing history. Actually, it was the most famous sporting event in history. Two undefeated champions.

A gladiatorial spectacle.

Like Adriana and Valentina, I'd only seen the fight (a thousand times) on tape, but I knew it backwards and forwards.

"Yeah, that Mercante was a bum," Valentina said dismissively. "That was definitely a knockdown in the eleventh round."

She was still mad about it.

In the eleventh round, Frazier dropped Ali to the canvas, but the referee (Arthur Mercante) didn't signal a knock down even though he should have. In the final and fifteenth round, however, there was never any question about the left hook that put Ali back on the canvas.

Unanimous decision.

So we talked a lot about boxing. What else? Especially the other great Philly fighters like Bernard Hopkins, Meldrick Taylor, Saad Muhammad, etc.

The girls really knew their stuff.

When they found out that I'd been contracted to do a book of sports quotes, they were all over it.

"Any Joe quotes?"

I dropped my favorite:

Courage is how bad you want it.

They nodded their approval.

"Yeah, got that right!" Adriana agreed.

Then Valentina pressed me for some more boxing stuff.

[Here, as requested (required), are seven classics quotes and seven personal favorites kicked off with my top three GOATs.]

The greatest boxers of all-time:

Joe Louis

Sugar Ray Robinson

Roberto Duran

[With respects to Greb, Pep, Armstrong, Ali, Hagler, and Pacquaio]

Classics quotes:

I'll moider da bum. (Two-Ton Tony Galento)

I can lick any man in the house. (John L. Sullivan)

We wuz robbed. (Manager Joe Jacobs after Schmeling's decision loss to Sharkey)

The bigger they come, the harder they fall. (Ruby Robert Fitzsimmons)

He's a credit to his race – the human race. (Jimmy Cannon on Joe Louis)

He can run, but he can't hide. (Joe Louis before fighting Billy Conn)

Kill the body, and the head will follow. (Sam Langford)

Personal favorites:

If you screw things up in tennis, it's 15-love. If you screw up in boxing, it's your ass. (Randall "Tex" Cobb)

Boxing is like sin. It's too popular to be abolished. (Dave Anderson)

Everyone has a plan until they get punched in the face. (Mike Tyson)

Bakeries have destroyed more boxers than wine, women, and song. (Jim Murray)

Never have so few taken so much from so many. (Saoul Mamby on boxing managers)

Three of my wives were very good housekeepers. After we got divorced, they kept the house. (Willie Pep)

They say that money talks, but the only thing it ever said to me was good-bye. (Joe Louis)

I even threw out a cinematic bonus:

I coulda been a contender. (Terry Malloy in On the Waterfront)

I've been collecting quotes ever since I was a kid, which is always a crowd-pleaser, and my Philly girls were no exception tonight.

At some point, as I was starting to feel my whiskey sours, I changed the subject.

"I nearly got killed tonight," I announced.

I'm not sure if I said it to incite some sympathy, but if that was my whiskey-addled intention, it worked.

"Oh, you poor thing!"

"Poor, baby! Tell us about it."

So I did.

Later, when we were all getting a bit too sloppy, I kissed them both long and hard on the mouth, waded through both levels of Salsa heaven, and exited out on 34th Street to wait for my Uber.

As I stood there in the cool slick city night, I texted the woman in Caracas who'd never responded to my previous text.

Are you my father's lover?

Let's see what she says to that.

If anything.

Then I texted my girlfriend Katie, trying not to sound too angry.

Where the hell are you!

Chapter 3

Sea Girt

(Sunday, 12/12/21)

The phone rang.

I immediately shut it off.

I'd been sleeping soundly in my family's cottage at the New Jersey shore, right on the ocean, not far from Sea Girt Light.

I could hear the waves.

Soothing, yet distracting.

With an undercurrent of death.

Eventually, I faced the fact that I'd never get back to sleep, so I sat up on the edge of my bed.

It all came back.

Hard.

I remembered that I could now be lying, battered beyond recognition, on a metal slab in some ugly Manhattan morgue. But I wasn't. I was still very much alive, and I had the distinct feeling that the kid who'd been driving the van had actually saved my life by swerving away at the last second.

Then I remembered trying not to think about it by knocking off seven whiskey sours at the Copa and playing the boxing blowhard with two fun girls from Philly. But maybe I was being too hard on myself. We all had a good time.

I stood up, a bit sore on my right side, but not that much.

The cottage was empty except for me.

I looked at the clock.

7:16.

I was wearing dark sweats with "Rutgers" across the chest. I've always been pretty lucky with hangovers, and this morning was no exception. I felt fine.

Physically, at least.

As always, I was immediately drawn to the ocean.

I slipped on some deck shoes, threw a black slicker over my shoulders, exited the back porch, and walked across the cold hard winter sand.

I've always loved the shore in the winter. When the world is grey, and the ocean is black. When the summer crowds are gone, and the sun is behaving itself. When the ocean breeze is cold and bracing.

Thirty-five years ago, a few weeks before I was born, my parents bought this little green wooden cottage. Which they bought for me. So their forthcoming child would be able to take intermittent restful breaks during his life and get away from everything and enjoy the ocean.

Which I've done throughout my life.

At the time of the purchase, they had no idea that Sea Girt, just north of Manasquan, would eventually be considered one of the more expensive ZIP codes in the country. They were also naturally unaware that their son would grow up to be a sportswriter, and that (ironically) Sea Girt had once been the home of New York Giants star and coach Alex Webster, as well as, years later, the home of Bill Parcells, also a one-time coach of the football Giants.

For whom we rooted.

Both of whom I got to know eventually, and both of whom were especially kind to the young kid who loved football and the football Giants but was really far more obsessed with baseball and boxing.

I walked down close to the ocean. The beach was empty in both directions. It was as if I was the last person on earth.

Naturally, I thought about death.

Which was something I'd done very little of in my life.

Which I suppose has been mostly a shallow life. Yeah, I go to church sometimes on Sunday, yeah, I believed what I'm supposed to believe (despite my constant transgressions), but I've never taken the time to think too deeply about the truly deep things. The truth is, ever since I graduated from Rutgers fifteen years ago, I haven't read a single book that wasn't a sports book.

I stared out at the dark Atlantic which seemed eternally black and dead, and I believed that I was thinking about death, but I was really thinking about judgment.

As best I could.

Last night, I definitely could have died, but if I had, let's face it, it would have been an easy death. It would have been over in a fraction of an instant, and it's highly probably that I wouldn't have felt any pain at all. Unlike so many other poor suffering people when they're dying.

But what about afterwards?

I remembered when I was a high school senior in Fr. Grady's theology class at St. Joe's High. Naturally, I was far too foolish to learn any theology, since I was probably daydreaming about sports the whole time, with endless stats racing through my stupid head. But I do remember that Fr. Grady always kept a quote posted high on the blackboard of his classroom. Up at the far right. Which I often stared at during class without any real comprehension.

Nevertheless, it was ingrained in my mind.

Always be thou prepared, and so live that death may never find thee unprepared.

Written by some guy named Thomas à Kempis.

Whomever that was.

Which really didn't matter.

So I stared at the black ocean and realized that I wasn't really thinking about death because I was really thinking about what happens afterwards.

About judgment.

And despite Thomas à Kempis's warning, I was totally unprepared.

I was burdened with sins, and I had nothing to show for myself but an essentially self-absorbed and frivolous life.

It was a shockingly hard admission.

One that was hard to face.

So I went back inside the old cottage and took off my raincoat.

What should I do with myself today?

I really didn't want to deal with Katie, who'd never even bothered to call me back. I was afraid that I'd get angry and say something unpleasant.

Actually, I didn't want to deal with anyone else either.

I looked over at my desk.

I also didn't feel like working on my stupid quote book.

What was the point anyway?

I stared at the quote I'd taped on the wall above my desk. It was a quote from Jimmy Cannon.

Sports is the toy department of life.

Yeah, exactly, Jimmy.

I've spent my whole life in a toy department.

Just like a child.

I went into the bathroom to wash my face. I splashed some water on myself then looked at the pathetic guy staring back at me. Tallish, a bit more than six feet, confident, not that hard to look at, especially considering the fact that the black van had swerved at the last minute and didn't crush his face to a bloody pulp. Sandy brown hair, deep blue eyes, the left one being dead and a bit glazed, usually covered with a black eye patch.

Not overall unappealing.

But who *was* this guy anyway?

I tried to be honest about it.

Half Scot-American, half Hungarian-American. An only child, great parents, father deceased. A bit of a loner, but many friends and colleagues. A lazy quasi-lapsed Catholic, a Jersey wiseass, sometimes a bit aloof. Sometimes a bit acerbic. Dresses casual (jeans, sweatshirts, sweaters, windbreakers, deck shoes), yet always wears a pristine dark suit to sporting events, even in the hot summer and the cold of winter. Mostly likeable, I guess. Definitely likes women, who, for some reason, seem to like him.

Probably a "decent" person overall.

But how does "decent" fly at one's death?

At one's judgment?

My phone vibrated.

I dried my face and walked back to my desk.

It was Lili calling again, so I ignored it and ignored her message.

Almost immediately, the thing vibrated again.

This time it was a text.

answer your phone!

The phone rang.

Fine, you win, Lili.

I picked it up, and she spoke in a rush.

"Do you know what's happened, Richie?"

She sounded peculiar, as if somehow wounded.

Something was clearly wrong.

"No, what are you talking about?"

"Katie's dead."

Since it didn't really register right away, I said nothing.

My mind was disordered.

Completely

"Are you still there, Richie?"

"Yes," I managed. "Are you sure?" I added stupidly.

"Yes."

"How?"

"Suicide."

I was suddenly overcome with physical weakness and sick to my stomach. I slumped down into my desk chair.

Was it possible?

Was Katie really dead?

Chapter 4

St. Ladislaus

(Sunday, 12/12/21)

I was staring at the guy's bronze statue.

Cardinal József Mindszenty.

He was once the Archbishop of Esztergom and the longtime leader of the Hungarian Catholic Church for three decades in the twentieth century. I knew his story well. My mother had made sure of that, and so had the priests at St. Ladislaus.

As an outspoken anti-socialist, he was arrested twice in 1919, the second time by Béla Kun's communist government. Twenty-five years later, he was arrested by the fascists for his opposition to the pro-Nazi Arrow Cross Party. After the conclusion of World War II, he was arrested by the communist Hungarian People's Party for alleged treason and espionage. Routinely tortured, Mindszenty was forced to confess (which he immediately recanted), then subjected to a show trial in 1949 and given a life sentence.

Seven years later, during the 1956 Hungarian Revolution, he was released from prison by the freedom fighters before the Soviet tanks rolled into Budapest and reestablished Hungary as a Soviet satellite state. Before he could be recaptured, Mindszenty was granted asylum at the US Embassy in Budapest where he lived for the next fifteen years. After a controversial agreement (compromise) between the Vatican and the People's Republic, Mindszenty was exiled from Hungary, living in Vienna until his death in 1975.

For many people, the cardinal became a powerful symbol of defiance against the twin evils of communism and fascism, as well as a world-admired defender of the Catholic faith. Two years ago in 2019, Pope Francis declare Cardinal Mindszenty "Venerable" in his continuing progression towards, hopefully, canonization.

As you can see, I was doing my best to try and distract myself from the incomprehensible death of my beautiful girlfriend Katie Kovacs. As soon as I got off the phone with Lili earlier, I drove up the Parkway heading towards New Brunswick.

I was numb, thinking of nothing but Katie.

Of her lovely ever-lively brown eyes.

Of the sweet, cute, adorable brunette, whom everyone loved. Who was fun, upbeat, personable, and unpretentiously smart as hell. We'd first met two years ago in 2020 at an evening reception at Citi Field for my recently published book *Amazin'* about the Miracle Mets. Katie was working PR for the Mets, and when I caught her smile across the room, I disengaged from whomever I was talking to, went right over, and asked her if I could dedicate my next book to her.

She laughed.

"Only if it's PG," she kidded.

"All my stuff is PG," I assured her.

"*Roids* gets pretty edgy at times," she pointed out with yet another smile.

She was definitely right about that. My book about the steroid scandal in baseball was, at times, a bit of a screed.

We soon discovered that we'd both grown up in New Brunswick, New Jersey, that we both had Hungarian heritages, and that we both went to the same parish. Even though I was ten years older than Katie, we knew lots of the same people.

There was even more.

We both went to Rutgers.

Me for journalism, Katie for sports management.

I got her another glass of Veuve Clicquot, and when I'd finished signing all the copies of *Amazin'* that I needed to sign, and when I'd finished talking to everyone that I needed to talk to, especially the '69 old-timer Mets who were present (Ed Kranepool, Cleon Jones, Jerry Koosman, and others), Katie and I went over to Valentino's until the place closed. Then I accompanied her back to Hoboken, where I'd once lived myself, and we settled into the all-night Malibu Diner, where we talked until five in the morning.

When I walked her back to her apartment downtown in the Railhead District, I kissed her at her front door.

She smiled.

"Yummy."

I didn't know what to say to that, but the feeling was more than mutual.

"Are you now my boyfriend?" she asked.

Once again I didn't know what to say, but I said something anyway.

"For as long as you want, Katie Kovacs."

And that was that.

Now I was sitting outside St. Ladislaus, my family's church, her family's church, staring at the rather imposing and rather intimidating bronze statue of the great Hungarian primate.

Much to my mother's delight, I was actually born on Mindszenty's birthday.

March 29.

1892 for him.

1986 for me.

At my First Holy Communion, my mother gave me a holy card of Cardinal Mindszenty, which I've carried in my wallet ever since.

Sunday Mass was finally letting out, and the parishioners were exiting the entrance doors of the old church founded in 1904.

When I'd arrived earlier, it was after 10:30, so I decided to wait outside. I was too much of a mess to do anything but stare at the bronze statue.

Eventually, Lili, dressed in a lovely forest green overcoat, came out beneath the gray skies. She was also a mess, and it was clear that she'd been crying.

Lili was Katie's closest cousin as well as her best friend since childhood. Like Katie and me, she grew up in New Brunswick with Hungarian heritage, and like Katie and me, she went to Rutgers. In her case, it was a business degree. After graduation, she decided to work at her father's trucking company, and she's now (age twenty-five) engaged to Eddie Crews, her high school boyfriend who works in construction.

For some reason, Lili has always liked me, and I'm not sure why. Most of Katie's family would have been pleased to see me make a fast exit from Katie's life, and the fact that I still hadn't proposed to Katie, or even discussed it, obviously pleased none of them.

Including Lili.

Which was now all moot.

She embraced me, and she held me close.

At first, we didn't say much.

Eventually, we went back inside the empty church and sat next to each other in the last pew. When Lili knelt down on the kneeler to say some prayers, I went over and lit a few candles, which was something my mother always liked to do.

"Never pass a church without lighting a prayer candle," she'd always say, and despite my mushy Catholicism I still never passed a church without stopping in to light a few. Sure, I know, at least for me, it was a lazy man's way of praying, but it was still a prayer, and I asked St. Margaret to comfort the soul of my lovely Katie.

Then I went back to the pew where Lili was now sitting.

Waiting.

"I don't believe it, Richie," she said softly.

She turned to look at me directly.

Intently.

"Do you?"

I knew what she meant.

She didn't mean that she couldn't believe that Katie was dead. That was apparently a certainty. She meant that she couldn't believe that it was suicide.

Neither could I.

"No."

It seemed impossible that a happy contented person like Katie would take her own life. I never saw any such indications. *None.* As far as I could see during the past two years, she was never depressed about anything. Not even me. Life for Katie, despite its natural irritations and disappointments, was always a beautiful thing. She was one of those truly unique people who enjoyed the life that God had given her, and she did the best with it that she possibly could.

"Why do they think it's suicide?" I asked.

I knew that they'd found her in her bed in her Hoboken apartment with an empty bottle of Zolpidem on her night table.

Sleeping pills.

Which seemed perfectly ridiculous and suspicious since I was never aware that Katie had any kind of sleeping issues.

Lili was hesitating.

"Tell me, Lili."

"There was a note."

I was incredulous.

"A note?"

"Yes, on her computer screen."

I was getting the feeling that the note was about me.

"What did it say?"

"It seems to blame you, Richie."

"What did it say?"

"It said, 'Forgive me, Richard.'"

"That's it? Three words?"

"That's it, but her parents think it's blaming you for stringing her along. For not taking her more seriously."

I was stunned.

But maybe I shouldn't have been.

"Are you buying any of this, Lili?"

"I don't know what to believe, Ritchie."

Which was hardly reassuring.

"Look at me, Lili."

She turned and looked.

"Do you think that Katie killed herself?"

"No," she shook her head. "No, I can't believe it."

"Then maybe it's not true."

She nodded thoughtfully.

"Yeah, maybe it's not."

Chapter 5

Lorain Street

(Sunday, 12/12/21)

"You seem off tonight, Richie."

It was a question not just a statement of fact.

My mom, who'd never smoked a day in her life, was lying and dying in her bed in our family home on Lorain Street in New Brunswick. Dying, inexplicably, of lung cancer. Oddly, statistically, twenty percent of the women who come down with this ugly disease are non-smokers, and the oncologists and the pulmonologists have no idea why it happens. They speculate about hormones, genetic mutations, and secondhand smoke (even though my old man never smoked either), but the truth is they don't have a clue. To make things even worse, she got the small-cell variety which is much quicker and much more lethal.

Naturally, I've wondered if it might have had something to do with all the years that she spent in the chem lab at Johnson & Johnson, but, again, my old man was also there in the very same lab.

I guess it's all moot now anyway, as my wonderful mother coughs, has trouble catching her breath, suffers chest pains, and has lost over fifteen pounds. She's also endured pulmonary surgery, chemo, radiation, and various experimental immunotherapies, with a final prognosis of death sometime within the next few weeks.

Or less.

It's perfectly horrible, and I've done my best to comfort her, which I'm sure is perfectly inadequate. Yet she seems fully accepting, strong in her faith, and believing that my old man, who died thirteen years ago, is patiently waiting for her somewhere.

So I never bothered to mention that her only son, her only child, nearly got squished to death last night in mid-Manhattan, and I also didn't tell her about Katie's suicide, even though I knew she'd find out soon enough from her many friends and priests at St. Ladislaus.

"I'm fine, Mom," I lied, which she knew was a lie, but she didn't press it. The drugs were making her drowsy anyway.

So I asked her what I shouldn't have asked her.

But I couldn't restrain myself.

"Did you ever meet any of those kids that Dad sponsored in South America?"

Naturally, it seemed like an odd question.

Out of left field.

After I was born, my father, as an act of gratitude, began sponsoring a number of impoverished kids down in South America through various Catholic relief agencies like the Christian Foundation for Children, now known simply as Unbound. Every month, he donated money to the parents of the children, and even though I never knew how many he was sponsoring at any given time, I was always under the impression that it was about fifteen or so. Since I'm thirty-five years old and my old man died thirteen years ago, that means that he was at it for about twenty-two years. In his will, he left each of those charitable agencies a sizable donation to continue his sponsorships until the kids aged out at eighteen years old. Which was standard policy.

"No, Richie, that was your father's pet project, and I never knew much about it."

I pressed ahead anyway.

"Does the name Inês ring any bells?"

"Not really. There were lots of kids over the years, both boys and girls. God bless them all."

As she blessed them all, she fell off to sleep.

Which looked like death to me.

My mom was sixty years old and despite her illness, she still looked lovely, with her always pretty face and her thick now-graying hair. In truth, I'd been blessed with marvelous parents, who were both loving and lovingly demanding at the same time, whom I naturally took for granted as a kid.

Soon I would be all alone in this world, without either one of them.

I got up and wandered to the back of the house and my old man's study, which my mom now refers to as the "Mets Room." My dad was a dedicated and world-class biochemist, but he was also a diehard Mets fan. On his desk at Johnson & Johnson, he had a baseball signed by Tom Seaver prominently displayed, and he always wore a Mets cap when working around the house. After his death, in his memory, I started filling up his study with Mets memorabilia. Stuff that I'd purchased from various auction houses and collectible companies. Admittedly, I went overboard. The room was now cluttered with signed baseballs, signed photographs, jerseys, pennants, bobbleheads, even some one-of-a-kind oddities like a special ashtray designed like Shea Stadium that Mets management had given to broadcaster Ralph Kiner on his retirement from broadcasting.

"What are you planning to do with all this junk?" my mom would ask with one of her amused "I give up" smiles.

I had no idea.

It was perfectly moronic.

I sat down in the midst of it.

I'm sure the shrinks would say it was an expression of my love for my old man.

A way to deal with my loss.

Hell, I'd agree with that.

So was the book.

I wrote *Amazin'* for my old man, and the book was dedicated to him and his memory. As a thirteen-year-old Jersey kid, he'd lived and breathed the Miracle Mets of 1969, and I wished that I'd been capable of completing the book before he died when I was still only twenty-two and just beginning to establish my bona fides as a reputable journalist and sports historian. By the time I finally started the project, I had seemingly unlimited resources (both personal and bibliographical), and all but a few of the still-surviving members of the legendary Mets of 1969 were more than willing to sit down and talk and remember.

There was a lot to remember.

It was the Mets eighth season as an expansion club in New York City, and to say that they'd been stinking up the joint during the previous seven years would be an outrageous understatement since they were always the worst or next-to-worst team in the National League. Then the magic happened in 1969 under the second-year management of Gil Hodges. After a typically slow start, the team went on a tear in May, but they were still ten games back of the Cubs in mid-August. Then they took off again in September and pulled off one of the biggest turnarounds in baseball history (known as the "collapse" in Chicago) and ended their season with a hundred wins, eight games ahead of the hapless Cubs. Then they easily beat the Braves in the NLCS and then beat the powerhouse Orioles in the World Series.

Even if you know nothing about baseball, you can see that it was an incredible story, and the team's post-regular-season was full of amazing performances, dazzling plays, and even oddities (like the famous "shoe polish" incident). The games showcased Mets legends like Tom Seaver (1969 Cy Young Award Winner and eventual Hall of Famer), young Nolan Ryan (eventually a Hall of Famer as well), Gil Hodges (hopefully soon to be a member of the Hall of Fame), Jerry Koosman, Ed Kranepool, Cleon Jones, Tommie Agee, Don Clendenon (World Series MVP), Ron Swoboda, etc.

The book was a sensation, and it made me a lot of money.

But I'd done it for my dad who'd always supported me.

Always.

"I want to do *that*," I'd told him categorically when I was fifteen years old.

Then I held up the *Post* so my old man could see the article by Phil Mushnick.

"A sportswriter?" he asked.

He seemed genuinely surprised, even though I was, unlike my parents, pretty much of a science moron, and even though they'd named me Richard Young Ramsey. Which was my old man's clever homage to his favorite sportswriter Dick Young. Apparently, my mom wasn't that crazy about the idea, so my father pointed out that "Young" was a distinguished surname on the Scot side of the family (his side), so she went along with it.

"Yeah, Dad, I'm not much good at anything else."

By that time, my eye had been blinded by a line drive at third base, and my grades had been floating perilously above average.

"Let me talk to your mother about it," he decided.

Which he did.

Later that night, he came into my room.

"If you do it, Richie, then you're going to do it right. Right?"

"Right."

So I went to work, which was really more like fun than work. While other kids were out playing ball or inside playing dumb video games, I was assiduously reading about all the great sportswriters, as well as reading their old columns and books.

For example:

Grantland Rice (1880-1954): The legend from Tennessee who ended up at the *New York Tribune*, covering the likes of Thorpe, Ruth, Dempsey, Bobby Jones, Rockne, and "The Four Horsemen of the Apocalypse," often romanticizing both athletes and sporting events in eloquent and elegant mellifluent prose.

A. J. Liebling (1904-1963): The Dean of Boxing Writers, a versatile author often associated with *The New Yorker,* who wrote *The Sweet Science* (1956), which was named the greatest sports book of all time by *Sports Illustrated.*

Red Smith (1905-1982): Another legend, Smith covered baseball, football, boxing, and horse racing for the *New York Herald Tribune* and the *New York Times,* he was the second sportswriter (of four) to win the Pulitzer Prize, a solid Joe Frazier man.

Jimmy Cannon (1909-1973): A New Yorker through and through who wrote for the *Daily News,* the *Post,* and the *Journal-American,* as well as serving as a war correspondent for *Stars and Stripes,* he famously wrote that "boxing is the red light district of sport," and he was eventually elected to the International Boxing Hall of Fame.

Jim Murray (1919-1998): Another recipient of the Pulitzer Prize, who modestly said that the award should have gone to someone who was writing consequential journalism about politics or economics, he wrote a popular nationally syndicated column for the *Los Angeles Times,* and he was also a regular columnist at *Sports Illustrated.*

Roger Angell 1920-): Harvard-educated fiction editor at *The New Yorker* who wrote literary essays about baseball that were collected in *The Summer Game* and *Five Seasons*.

Roger Kahn (1927-2020): NYU grad at the *New York Herald Tribune* and the *Saturday Evening Post*, who wrote *The Boys of Summer*, which placed second on *Sports Illustrated*'s list of "The Top 100 Sports Books of All Time" after *The Sweet Science*.

Dave Anderson (1929-2018): Another Pulitzer winner, he wrote for the *New York Journal-American* and the *New York Times*, and he was a member of the International Boxing Hall of Fame and the recipient of the Nat Fleischer Award for excellence in boxing journalism.

Not to mention my all-time favorite:

Dick Young (1917-1987): the hard-hitting sports dean of the New York *Daily News* for forty-five years, the first reporter to invade the previously sacrosanct team locker rooms, sometimes called vicious, brash, cynical, abrasive, acerbic, and controversial, but always the very best sports read, it was Young who wanted to put an asterisk on Roger Maris's sixty-one homers, who was outraged that Willie Mays only got ninety-four percent of the Hall of Fame ballots (since some idiot writers believed that no one should get into the Hall on their first ballot), who had feuds and/or wars with Muhammad Ali, (while loving Joe Frazier), Jim Bouton, Howard

Cosell, and even Tom Seaver, he was also an outspoken critic of baseball's segregation policy and a longtime advocate for women sportswriters.

So I read these guys assiduously and many others as well. I certainly didn't agree with them all, but I still appreciated them all, and I'd like to believe that I've learned something useful from each and every one of them. As for more contemporary writers, there are far too many to mention (many of whom are friends or colleagues, although some are definitely *not* friends), but I can't resist mentioning hardass Phil Mushnick at the New York *Post*, as well as Tony Kornheiser and Michael Wilbon on *PTI*, which I watch religiously every single weekday.

So my old man informs me that he'll buy me all the books that I need and that he'd pay for selected sporting event tickets (within reason), but that I have to establish some kind of personal resolution for myself.

Some kind of code.

Which we created together.

When I was fifteen.

In which I vowed to do my best to be morally responsible and to always put my readers first (even though I didn't have any readers yet). That I would be honest and professional. That I would triple-check all my facts. That I would write clearly and logically and never pretentiously. That I would be a good colleague and that I would never let any successes that I might have go to my head.

Then he made me write it all down (I still have it) as my "Statement of Intention." At the bottom of the page, my father wrote a line from a famous prayer by St. Francis de Sales, the patron of writers and journalists.

Do not look forward in fear to the changes in life.

Good advice, but not so easy to do.

Every year on my birthday, I reread my "Statement," and I try to honestly evaluate where I've gone wrong and what I've done right. If I do have an overriding flaw, it's ironically the same one as Dick Young. I can, on occasions, get a bit high-handed. A bit caustic. Sometimes I have trouble containing my anger about stuff like drugs, cheating, tampering, showboating, greed, off-field violence against women, etc.

When *Roids* came out (my book about baseball's steroid scandal), my mom wasn't happy that I'd used certain crudities like "scumbags" and "shitheads," and my father agreed.

So do I.

My cell rang.

I was still sitting within my "toy department."

It was a text from Irene.

Guess what, Richard Ramsey? Little Eddie is yours!

Surely I was somehow beyond shock. I'd nearly died twenty-four hours ago, my girlfriend had supposedly committed suicide, one of my father's old lovers had resurfaced, and my mom was dying down the hallway.

Was it possible?

Was I losing my mind?

Was Irene's young child really mine?

I did the math in my head.

The kid was about five months old, and I'd been with Irene fourteen months ago after the final game of the NLCS between the Braves and the Dodgers in Arlington, Texas.

The math worked!

It was terrifying!

Did I really have a child?

With Irene Beckett?

With the likes of Irene Beckett?

I texted back the kind of question that any dumb male would have asked in such a situation.

Are you sure?

I waited.

There was no response.

Chapter 6

Jersey Detections

(Monday, 12/13/21)

"**I** never expected to see *you* again!"

I was standing in the midst of Mack Dawson's cluttered office in a Newark strip mall.

"I need your help, Mack."

He stood up, and we shook hands.

The guy was huge. At least six-foot-seven, at least 285 pounds. Several years ago, not long after my divorce, my cousin Rebeka told me that someone seemed to be stalking my ex-wife Cindy. I was definitely out of the picture at the time (still am), but I still wanted to help out, to try and do something about it, so I called Jack Colt's office in Paterson, NJ. Since Colt is the most famous private detective in the metro area, I really didn't think he'd be interested in a stalking case, but I still decided to start at the top.

Maybe I'd get a good referral.

When I dialed, some tough old Jersey woman answered the phone.

"What do you want?"

I have to admit, I was taken aback. Stunned. Did she always answer the phone like that?

"I'd like to hire Mr. Colt," I tried.

"Yeah, you and everybody else with a problem within two hundred miles."

How do you respond to that?

Since I didn't know, I didn't respond.

She continued anyway.

"So what's *your* problem, pal?"

I felt ashamed admitting to the truth.

"Someone's stalking my ex-wife."

"Has he killed her yet?"

"No," I said weakly.

"Then call me back when he does."

Then I started wondering if this was her special brand of humor. Everyone knows that Jerseyites are a tough crowd, but this woman was way over the top.

She responded to my dead air.

"Besides, Johnny's out of town anyway."

Which I assumed was her pet name for her boss.

I couldn't resist.

"Just out of curiosity, why didn't you tell me that right away."

"Because I was lonely, and I thought I might enjoy our conversation."

Amused yet frustrated, I pressed ahead.

"Any suggestions?"

"Yeah, Mack Dawson, in Newark."

"Thanks."

"Have an interesting day, sonny."

Click.

So I called up Mack, and he and his staff started surveilling Cindy over the next three months.

Finding nothing.

"Sorry, Mr. Ramsey, but the only one stalking your ex was me."

It was obvious that Mack felt bad about it, but I felt certain that he'd done his best. He'd been recommended by Jack Colt's office, so I'd paid him well.

Now he was ready and willing to make up for what he felt was his failure ten years ago, so I told him about Katie's death and that I didn't believe it was a suicide.

"The boyfriend never does," he warned me.

"I know, but I still want to look into it."

"Fine, I'll get a copy of the police report, and we can go from there."

"Can you get it today? I'd like to see her body tomorrow morning before it's sent back to New Brunswick. She's in the morgue at Hoboken Medical Center."

He seemed surprised by my request, but he didn't discourage me.

"Sure, Mr. Ramsey, I think I can hustle up the necessary paperwork."

By which I assumed that he meant bogus paperwork, which was fine with me.

We shook hands again.

I liked the big guy. He was earnest, and from all accounts, he was both honest and capable.

I exited Jersey Detections and sat in my black Audi A7 in the strip mall's crowded parking lot. I'd learned earlier in the *Post* that the kid who'd nearly killed me last night at the Garden had coded on the way to the hospital. My guess is that he was already dead at the scene. His name was Carlos Molina. He was a seventeen-year-old from Hell's Kitchen, and he'd probably saved my life before he'd lost his own. The short *Post* article offered no reason why the kid's van had careened out of control. It was "currently under investigation."

But in truth I have to admit that I wasn't really thinking about the kid, or about my mom, or about Katie, or about Inês from Caracas. I was thinking about Irene Beckett.

Was I really the father of her young child?

A child I'd only seen in a few Facebook pictures last night.

Was it possible?

After her original text, Irene hadn't responded to any of my subsequent texts or emails, and she also wasn't picking up the phone when I called.

Irene was a sports stringer for the *Washington Post*, and I'd run into her two years ago at Nationals Park when I was down in DC covering the National's unlikely playoff run and their World Series victory in 2019. I suppose it would be fair to say that we'd seduced each other with alacrity. Irene was almost thirty, a knockout, and unhappily married to some bigshot neurologist. We met at the Rocklands BBQ concessions stand, and we slept together later that night at the Westin Washington in downtown DC.

In my own inadequate defense, Irene was hard if not impossible to resist, and for some reason she wanted me. Maybe because I was easy. After all, she could have had any guy in the stadium. She was (and still is) sultry as hell, with long dark hair, dark miss-nothing eyes, and poutish lips. Trim but not too trim, exotic, and incessantly radiating sexual heat. She was also smart, cynical, and fun, but certainly not happy to have ended up trapped in a hollow mansion in Great Falls, Virginia, with some guy whom she said "bored her to death."

She looked up from her tray.

From her pulled pork sandwich and her mac 'n cheese.

Her dark eyes fixed on me.

"You're Richard Ramsey," she decided.

"Thanks, I was wondering who I was."

"I've got your books," she smiled, "but I've never bothered to read them."

I played along.

"Yeah, why waste the time?"

She looked me over and made up her mind.

"Why don't we sit together, or better yet, I can sit on your lap."

It went like that until the final out.

Later there was lots of booze and sex.

The following year, I met her again after the seventh and final game of the NLCS in which the Dodgers beat the Braves 4-3 behind a home run-robbing catch by Mookie Betts in the fifth inning, a go-ahead homer by Cody Bellinger in the seventh inning, and quality relief from Julio Urías. Due to the Covid pandemic, the game was played at a neutral site, Globe Life Field in Arlington, Texas, with a limited number of fans in the stands. But all the sportswriters were there, including the DC knockout (yeah, I know I've already used that word, but it's perfectly accurate and Irene likes it a lot) from the *Washington Post*. Almost immediately after we'd run into each other again, we ended up in bed again. This time at the Four Seasons Resort in Las Colinas. And just like the first time, there was plenty of booze, mostly tequila.

I'm not proud of it, but it was many years after my divorce from Cindy and about a month before I met Katie.

Ever since that night in Arlington, Texas, I hadn't seen or heard from Irene again.

Until she texted me yesterday.

In truth, *all* of my past relationships (all with unmarried women) were similar failures, even the ones that lasted for a few months. Which was always my fault, for all the usual reasons: too busy, not attentive enough, distracted, even disinterested, and so on. I was admittedly a fundamentally lousy boyfriend. I'd done my best with Cindy (or what I thought was my best), and I'd never strayed during our one-year marriage, but it had ended like all my other relationships. Once it had ended, of course, I regretted it, and I tried to get her to reconsider, but she'd had enough.

I couldn't blame her.

Then I tried to do better with Katie, but I was just kidding myself.

But at least I'd been faithful.

Regardless, sometimes it was still hard to look at myself.

Especially now.

I'm the worthless idiot who might have been the father of a kid with another man's wife.

Sometimes I make myself sick to my stomach.

Chapter 7

Rutgers

(Monday, 12/13/21)

I was reading my Wiki page.

Distracting myself.

I have no idea who actually writes these things, but I check mine every year or so, just to remind myself who I am. Today seemed like a good day for that, given that I was as f-upped as anyone on the planet.

Born: March 29, 1986 (age 35)
New Brunswick, New Jersey, US
Alma Mater: Rutgers University (NJ), 2006
Employer: *Newark Star-Ledger* (2008-2010),
Sports Illustrated (2010-2019), Freelance (2019-)
Spouse: Cindy Sinclair Ramsey (2009-2010)

Richard Young Ramsey (born March 29, 1986) is an American sportswriter and sports historian who covers various sports but specialies in baseball and boxing. Currently freelance, he has previously worked at the *Newark Star-Ledger* and *Sports Illustrated*.

Early Life

Ramsey was born and raised in New Brunswick, New Jersey. He is the only child of biochemist Richard Ramsey and bio-technician Frances Molnar Ramsey, who served as her husband's lab director at Johnson & Johnson. He attended St. Joseph High School in Metuchen New Jersey, an all-boys Roman Catholic college prep. He was very active in sports until he was struck in the left eye and blinded by a line drive while playing third base for St. Joe's Falcons. He then began writing a sports column for *The Falcon*, the school's award-winning newspaper. After graduation, he attended Rutgers University for journalism and graduated in December 2006.

Career

While still at Rutgers, Ramsey secured an internship at the *Newark Star-Ledger* and was able to cover the New York Mets 2007 season and the team's disastrous pennant collapse. During the same year, he published an editorial in the *Star-Ledger* entitled "Mr. Wright and Mr. Juice," a scathing comparison between Mets all-star third-baseman David Wright and San Francisco Giants outfielder Barry Bonds, who was in the process of setting steroid-enhanced home run records. The editorial, which was reprinted nationally, led to a follow-up editorial, "Mr. Commissioner and the Juice Heads," which called for the immediate resignation of Baseball Commissioner Bud Selig for "looking the other way" regarding the widespread use of performance-enhancing drugs by MLB players. As a result of both controversial articles and his coverage of the Mets disappointing season, Ramsey unexpectedly received the 2007 Sportswriter of the Year Award from the American Association of Sportswriters (AAS), and in 2008, he was promoted to a full-time position at the *Star-Ledger*.

In 2009, Ramsey made the unusual choice of chronicling the exploits of New Jersey high school phenom, Mike Trout, and he also published, to much acclaim, his first book *Roids* about Baseball's Steroid Era. In 2012, he published *Fight of the Century*, a *Times* bestseller, about the legendary boxing match at Madison Square Garden in 1971 between undefeated heavyweight champions Joe Frazier and Muhammed Ali. In 2016, he covered the Rio Olympics on special assignment for *Sports Illustrated*, and two years later he published *Amazin'* about the 1969 Miracle Mets, which also became a *New York Times* bestseller. Ramsey is currently working on a book about the Houston Astros cheating scandal of 2017-2018.

<u>Personal Life</u>

Ramsey married Cindy Sinclair of Millville, New Jersey, in 2009, and they divorced the following year. He currently resides in New Brunswick, New Jersey.

Which is partially incorrect.

I was no longer "currently" writing a book about the Astros cheating scandal. I'd bagged that idea a while ago.

I'm not exactly sure why.

I shut off my phone.

I was sitting on a black iron bench beneath Willie the Silent on Voorhees Mall. I used to come here all the time when I was a Rutgers undergraduate over fifteen years ago. The Vorhees Mall, which runs from Old Queens to the Willie statue, is the bucolic hub of the main campus, a long stretch of lawn surrounded by old campus buildings and shaded by high hovering trees. In December, of course, the leaves were gone, and the green had faded from the grass, but it was still lovely. I suppose that when I came here years ago, I had big hopes and dreams for my future. Now I was living that future – as a successful sports-writer – and I was a total mess, both personally and professionally.

I looked up at old Willie. Back in my Rutgers days, I had no idea who the guy was. Just some European prince. But Katie, who'd been an RU undergrad ten years after me, once told me all about the old guy. Apparently William of Orange, the "Father of the Fatherland," had led a Dutch revolt against their Spanish occupiers which resulted in something called the Eighty Years War and eventually resulted in Netherlands independence.

"What's that got to do with Rutgers?" I asked her three years ago when we were sitting right here in Willie's bluestone plaza.

"Because, dumbbell, Rutgers was founded in 1766 as a Dutch-re-formed college originally called Queen's college, in the same way that Columbia had been named King's College twelve years earlier."

"Was Columbia Dutch-Reformed?"

"No, mostly Anglican."

Not that I understood the difference.

At some point, some guy from New York City had donated the imposing fifteen-foot bronze statue which rested atop a six-foot high stone base at the west end of Vorhees Mall. For nearly a hundred years, the statue has been the iconic heart of the campus, serving as the site of numerous protests, pep rallies, graduation ceremonies, festivals, and various acts of childish vandalism by our idiot one-time football rivals from down at Princeton. We won the very first game in that rivalry, of course, which was also the very first collegiate football game ever played. Back in 1869. Then Princeton had the upper hand for the next hundred years until we beat them five times in a row, and they quietly dropped us from their schedule.

Should I hesitate to use the word "cowards"?

Regardless, Willie the Silent, above all else, was a quiet comfortable place for countless generations of Rutgers students to come and think and relax beneath the high shading trees.

Today I was thinking, but not relaxing.

Thinking of Katie.

Last week, I'd bought her two upfront tickets for the upcoming Harry Connick concert at the Basie on February 4. It was intended to be an early Valentine's Day gift.

Now what should I do with them?

Maybe I should send them to Cindy?

Cindy, just like Katie, just like all women (it seems to me), loves Harry Connick.

Maybe I could send them anonymously.

Yeah, why not?

Chapter 8

Johnson & Johnson

(Monday, 12/13/21)

"How's your mom?"

I was sitting in the office of Dr. Kimberly Kim, the head of J&J's Infectious Diseases Division. Korean-born and now fifty-eight years old, Dr. Kim was a longtime colleague of my father and a close pal of my mom. She was brilliant, hard-working, likeable, and contentedly married with three adult children, all of whom were scientists.

When I was a kid I used to run around these hallways, in and out of the many offices and even some of the labs (although some were forbidden and locked), and I'd always called her Kim-Kim. Then, when I got a bit older, she became Kimmy. Eventually she became Dr. K.

I decided to be honest.

"Not the best."

She nodded and thought it over.

"I'd like to come over tonight, Richie Is that a good idea?"

"Sure, but don't mention my visit."

Which surprised her.

"Why not?"

"Because I need to ask you a question."

Although curious, she waited patiently.

"Did my father have a Latin lover?"

At first she looked at me like I was an idiot. Then like I was pranking her. Then, when she realized I was serious, she laughed.

"That's ridiculous, Richie. Your father was the most monogamous man I've ever met."

I didn't give up.

"You never had any suspicions?"

"None, no, never!"

She said it in a way that seemed to put an end to the idea, and I believed that she believed exactly what she was saying.

But I knew better.

Thirteen years ago, after my old man had died of heart failure, I emptied out his study since my mom was too distraught to deal with it. In one of his desk drawers, I found all of his sponsoree stuff, which was mostly his contracts with the agencies and various photos of the kids he'd sponsored. Also included was a photo of an older girl. A very beautiful girl, actually maybe a young woman, maybe eighteen or so, with no identifications except for six words neatly written in black ink near the bottom of the photograph.

Com todo o meu amor! Inês

I'm lousy with all foreign languages, including Spanish, but it didn't take a genius to figure it out. At the time, I was already dealing as best I could with my father's unexpected death, and now there was a new and even sicker feeling deep in my stomach.

I went to his computer and searched through his emails for Inês. There was one.

From 1996:

Yes, it was the best night of my life. Love, always, Inês

Which seemed to indicate that there'd been other related emails that had likely been deleted.

So what does a son who admired (even worshipped) his father do with that? Well, *this* son did what he always does with the ugly stuff in life. He buried it. I did my best to forget about it, and since there was no one whom I could talk to about it, I let it go.

But now Inês, whoever the hell she was, was back, and it was obvious that Dr. K. was a dead end.

"Where would you ever get such a ridiculous idea, Richie?"

I shrugged.

Attempting to shrug it off.

"Pay no attention, Kimmy. I'm a mess right now."

She understood. After all, my mom was dying.

I hadn't even bothered to tell her about Katie.

Not yet.

"Your father was a remarkable man," she remembered softly, almost to herself.

She was right about that.

My old man was born in the Bronx to Scot-American parents, and he seems to have been a science prodigy right from the get-go. At some point, he read Selman Waksman's autobiography, *My Life with Microbes*, and he wanted to be just like Waksman.

Who was obviously an excellent role model for someone to emulate.

Waksman was the legendary biochemist at Rutgers who discovered Streptomycin, the first effective medical treatment for tuberculosis, which saved countless lives worldwide. Waksman also coined the term "antibiotics," discovered over fifteen other antibiotic strains, and received the Nobel Prize in 1952.

So my father devoured Waksman's book and worked especially hard so he could go to Rutgers and study with his hero. Unfortunately, Waksman died in 1973 when my father was still in his junior year at Bronx Science. Nevertheless, when he finished high school, he went to Rutgers anyway, where he was soon working at the university's illustrious Waksman Institute of Microbiology, eventually completing his doctorate in 1980. Already a nationally distinguished microbiologist, my old man took a research position at nearby Johnson & Johnson where he met my mom who was a young lab tech at the time and who ended up both his wife and the director of his immunology lab, where they worked together, sometimes in conjunction with Dr. Kim, on various new strains of antibiotics.

My old man never won the Nobel like his hero Waksman, but his work saved untold numbers of lives (especially those stricken with Typhus and Dengue Fever) and alleviated the sufferings of many more.

Whereas his son had become a dumb-ass sportswriter.

While his father had been a man who'd successfully dedicated his life to curing diseases and mitigating human suffering.

Needless to say, I was always proud of my old man, and I felt guilty thinking that he might have, at some point in his life, betrayed my mother.

I changed the subject.

"How are things here at the factory?"

Which is what my old man always called the research labs at J&J.

"Very good right here, Richie, but, of course, not so good over in marketing."

Yeah, I was glad that my old man missed most of that.

All the lawsuits.

All the scandals.

J&J had been a shining light in health care ever since its founding in 1886 by Robert Wood Johnson. Famous for all kinds of health aids (especially sterilized adhesive Band-Aids), the company eventually grew into a multinational corporation with 250 subsidies located in sixty countries. Which is how the problems began, especially with the company's expansion and diversification in the Nineties.

Earlier in 1982, J&J had been universally praised for the way it handled (with immediate recall and widespread media alerts) the crisis in Chicago when some monster (still never caught) laced Tylenol capsules with cyanide and killed seven people. Nevertheless, by the 2000's, the corporate center in New Brunswick had seemingly lost control of its innumerable branches and products. There were endless lawsuits about Propulsid, contaminated Motrin, defective hip implants, Retin-A cream, Natrecor, and Risperdal. Most concerning were the charges that J&J subsidiary Janssen Pharmaceuticals improperly promoted painkillers that contributed to the opioid epidemic.

Equally disturbing were claims (cited in nearly forty thousand lawsuits) that the talc in the company's popular Baby Powder had caused ovarian cancers, which the company still denies.

The result of all of this was billions of dollars paid out in court cases, as well as the demeaning of the good name of a distinguished American institution that had done as much for pain relief and health care as any company in world history.

So, yeah, I was glad that my old man had missed most of it, but Dr. Kim had seen it all, even though it had never affected her own invaluable research.

"Is the company getting a handle on it?" I asked.

"I think they are. I certainly hope so. Problems always arise when expansions happen too quickly, and those problems have affected people's lives. It's a serious concern for all of us who work here."

Since it was a hard and unpleasant subject, I left it right there.

So did Kimmy.

She pointed over at her bookshelf, and I could see the spines of my four books standing in the midst of all her incomprehensible medical texts.

"Your dad would have been very proud of *Amazin'*. It's a truly amazing book!"

"Thanks, Kimmy, that really means a lot. I just wish I could have written the book before he died."

"Well, I'm sure he's read it."

Which was a peculiar image.

My old man reading a sports book somewhere in the afterlife.

In heaven.

Kimberly Kim was a serious Christian and a serious Catholic, but she was also, just like my father, a sports fanatic, with season passes to both the Jets and the Knicks.

"So what are you working on now?"

"Knopf wants me to do a book of sports quotes. They made a ton of money off my nicknames book, and they're hoping to do it all over again."

"I love the idea, Richie! Any Joe quotes?"

By whom she meant Joe Namath, whose signed photo was framed on her wall to my right.

"Of course."

"Try me."

I gave her two, both of which she surely knew word for word.

I've got news for you. We're gonna win the game. I guarantee it. (Before winning Super Bowl IV)

I can't wait until tomorrow 'cause I get better looking every day.

She laughed, and she asked for more.

[Here goes, as requested.]

The greatest football players of all-time:

Jim Brown

Johnny Unitas

Peyton Manning

[With respects to Montana, Taylor, Brady, White, Rice, and Mahomes]

Classic quotes:

When the going gets tough, the tough get going. (Bear Bryant)

Winning isn't everything; it's the only thing. (Vince Lombardi)

Football doesn't build character. It eliminates the weak ones. (Darrell Royal)

If it doesn't matter who wins or loses, then why do they keep score? (Vince Lombardi)

Football is not a contact sport; it's a collision sport. Dancing is a contact sport. (Duffy Daugherty)

Show me a good loser, and I'll show you a loser. (Vince Lombardi)

If you're a pro coach, NFL stands for "not for long." (Jerry Glanville)

Personal favorites:

Losing the Super Bowl is worse than death. With death you don't have to get up the next morning. (George Allen)

The reason women don't play football is because eleven of them would never wear the same outfit in public. (Phyllis Diller)

The Bears are so tough when they finish sacking the quarterback, they go after his family in the stands. (Tim Wrightman)

If a man watches three football games in a row, he should be declared legally brain dead. (Erma Bombeck)

When he goes on safari, the lions roll up their windows. (Monte Clark on Larry Csonka)

If God wanted women to understand men, football would never have been created. (Roger Simon)

If me and King Kong went into an alley, only one of us would come out. And it wouldn't be the monkey. (Lyle Alzado)

Then she asked about basketball.

Naturally.

[So here we go again.]

The greatest basketball players of all-time:

Wilt

Abdul-Jabbar

Jordan

[With respects to Magic, Bird, Duncan, James, Curry, and Mikan]

Classic quotes:

Bad shooters are always open. (Pete Carril)

Not only is there more to life than basketball, there's a lot more to basketball than basketball. (Phil Jackson)

There's no "I" in team, but there is in win. (Tex Winter and Michael Jordan)

The strong take from the weak, and the smart take from the strong. (Pete Carril)

A tough day at the office is even tougher when your office contains spectator seating. (Nik Posa)

I don't know why people question the academic training of a student athlete. Half the doctors in the country graduated in the bottom half of their class. (Al McGuire)

My responsibility is getting all my players playing for the name on the front of the jersey, not the one on the back. (Anonymous)

Personal favorites:

We can alley, but we don't have the oop. (Abe Lemons)

We have a great bunch of outside shooters. Unfortunately, all our games are played indoors. (Weldon Drew)

What do you have when you have an agent buried up to his neck in sand? Not enough sand. (Pat Williams)

There are really only two plays: "Romeo and Juliet" and put the darn ball in the basket. (Abe Lemons)

I want my teams to have my personality – surly, obnoxious, and arrogant. (Al McGuire)

Basketball has so much showboating you'd think it was invented by Jerome Kern. (Art Spander)

If cocaine were helium, the NBA would float away. (Art Rust)

When I'd worn her out with enough sports quotes, I hit her with an unrelated question.

"Who's the best pathologist in New Jersey?"

She was naturally surprised, but she answered without hesitation.

"Aaron Ehrlich. He's over at Beth Israel. Why?"

I ignored her "why."

"Would he do you a favor?"

"I believe he would, Richie. What's up?"

So I told her what was up.

I told her about Katie Kovacs.

Chapter 9

Hoboken Medical Center

(Tuesday, 12/14/21)

The morgue smelled like a morgue.

At least, what I imagined a morgue would smell like. Cool and chemical-ish, with a hint of death.

We were down in the bowels of St. Mary's, the second oldest hospital in New Jersey, now known as Hoboken University Medical Center, looking down at the dead body of my girlfriend.

Naked on a metal slab, partially covered with a white sheet.

"You all right?" Mack checked.

"Yeah," I said, more numb than all right.

She looked paler than usual. Maybe that was to be expected. Maybe it was the lighting. She was inert and lifeless, but still very pretty, and I was overwhelmed with sorrow, sorrow that I hadn't done more to make her happy.

"May I?" Dr. Ehrlich asked the young morgue attendant whose name was Dubcek.

"Of course."

The young guy was obviously in awe of Ehrlich, and I knew why because I'd googled the old boy this morning. Dr. Aaron Ehrlich was the former Essex County Medical Examiner and Coroner, and he was a legend throughout the metro area. Currently in his eighties, he'd performed over a thousand autopsies, and he'd served as an expert witness in several hundred court cases not only in New Jersey, but in New York and many other states. If you wanted someone to check out a dead body in New Jersey, Ehrlich was your guy.

We were here this morning, of course, under false pretenses. Mack had arranged our visit on the basis of some suspect documents that were surely bogus, which allowed Dr. Ehrlich to examine the body before it was autopsied and sent to the funeral home in New Brunswick.

Apparently, in Essex County, every assumed suicide is routinely autopsied.

The old doctor pulled back the white sheet, uncovering everything.

It was very unsettling, but I didn't want to leave the room.

Then I noticed something immediately.

"What's that?"

The old coroner, who was examining Katie's head, turned to look at me.

"What?"

"Katie never wore dark nail polish like that."

It was a deep shade of purple.

Ehrlich silently stepped to his left and lifted up Katie's left hand. Gently. Then he looked over at the attendant.

"I'm sure that Dr. Candara will observe the injection puncture beneath the nail on the left forefinger, but you might as well alert him anyway."

He was being diplomatic.

As for what had just happened, I think I saw it once in some old movie. A killer injects some kind of deadly toxin beneath the victim's fingernail. In this case, the killer even took the time to carefully recoat Katie's fingernails with the wrong color.

Everything had happened too quickly.

Too easily.

I looked over at Dubcek.

"Will Dr. Candara run toxicology tests?"

It was a stupid question, and I probably hadn't even worded it correctly, but the young attendant was understanding. Polite and considerate. I guess he'd figured, given my behavior, that I was Katie's boyfriend or brother or husband or something like that.

"Yes, he'll do a thorough scan," he assured me.

"I'm sure he will," Dr. Ehrlich agreed.

Then it hit me hard.

A debilitating wave of nausea.

With complete enervation.

With a terrible loneliness.

As I started to collapse, Mack grabbed me and held me up.

"There are chairs right outside," Dubcek suggested with some urgency as Mack helped me from the room and set me down in a chair in the outside corridor.

Nothing like that had ever happened to me before.

I guess, given the circumstances, it made a lot of sense.

Eventually, I came back to myself.

"You all right, kid?"

In Mack's world, I was still a "kid."

"I'm good," I said weakly.

Then I looked directly at Mack.

"But some f-upped bastard murdered my girlfriend!"

Chapter 10

Moore's Funeral Home

(Tuesday, 12/14/21)

No one was happy to see me.

No one.

Naturally.

What else did I expect?

After all, I was the bastard who'd strung along their princess.

Who was also *my* princess.

Fortunately, the room was large and crowded, and I did my best to be inconspicuous.

Earlier, I'd gone up to the coffin to see the body and say a prayer.

A prayer to St. Elizabeth of Thuringia, her favorite saint.

She looked very different than she had this morning in Hoboken. Since that time, she'd been autopsied, shipped to New Brunswick, and prepped for the viewing. Now wearing make-up. Now wearing the pretty light-blue Ralph Lauren dress she always loved.

Which I loved as well.

I overheard several people remarking how beautiful she looked, but she seemed more real to me this morning in the morgue. Yes dead and exposed, but still lovely. Now she seemed a bit made up. A bit like a doll. With too much make-up.

Besides, I knew that her inners had been all cut up, and I tried to put it out of my mind.

Eventually, of course, I had to go over to her devastated parents. Mrs. Kovacs did her best to be welcoming, even giving me a warmish hug, but I knew what she was thinking, assuming that she was thinking about me at all. Here was the selfish self-absorbed guy who'd wasted the last two years of Katie's life. Who was, admittedly, kind to her, but not in the most important ways. Who'd probably been the reason for her daughter's suicide.

The cause.

Even though I now knew that there'd never been a suicide.

As for Katie's father, he shook my hand.

That was it.

There was no pretense, and, in truth, I couldn't blame him.

Or any of the family for that matter.

Yes, I wanted to tell them all, everyone present, that Katie hadn't taken her own life. That some evil monster had murdered their precious Katie, but Mack had warned me not to say a word.

"Let the police handle it, Richie. Don't get involved."

Well, I was already involved, but I knew what he meant because as soon as the cops start to investigate, I'll be suspect number one, even though I've never touched a hypodermic needle in my entire life.

So even if I did walk up to the coffin and announce to all of her family and all of her friends the "good news" that Katie didn't kill herself, it still wouldn't change the fact that Katie was dead. That her life was over and done. And that the guy making the announcement would suddenly transition from being the bastard who'd hurt her so bad that she took her own life to the bastard who'd probably injected some toxic crap into her bloodstream and killed her.

So I said nothing and wandered around the room, wishing that I was somewhere else, talking to whoever wished to speak with me since there were a few mutual friends who wanted to say something nice to the dead girl's suffering boyfriend, unaware that everyone else assumed that I was the cause of her death.

Worn out, I found the men's room.

To hide.

To distract myself, I searched for more information about the dead kid who hadn't killed me in front of the Garden three nights ago.

There was now an obituary.

Carlos Molina, seventeen, was from a close-knit Puerto Rican family in Hell's Kitchen on West Forty-Ninth Street. He was the oldest of five children in a Catholic family, and a junior at Regis High School. An honor student and the vice-president of his class, he also played third base on the Owl's baseball team and dedicated his free time to young kids at the PAL Duncan Center on Fifth-Second Street. He was planning to attend St. John's next fall on a "full ride" as a bio major.

He also worked three nights a week as an Uber driver to help out his family.

He was "the light of our lives."

Lots of families say nice stuff when a kid dies, but this kid seemed exceptional in every way. He seemed like a much better kid than I ever was.

I shut off my phone.

I'd had enough for one day, and it was time to get the hell out of this deathtrap. But out in the hallway, I ran into some of the Kovacs relatives, including the Sykes brothers, Bryan and Colin, who were Katie's maternal Irish cousins. I always thought they were boring blowhards, and they never liked me either.

They came over aggressively and blocked my path.

"What were you doing at the morgue, asshole?" Bryan asked.

I was surprised that he knew, and I wondered what else he knew, but for the moment I just wanted to get myself out of the funeral parlor.

"I needed to see her," I said, without explanation.

Then Randy came over.

Randy Pierce had never made the slightest pretense that he was willing to try and like me. I guess I couldn't blame him. He was Katie's ex-boyfriend, her high school sweetheart, and he got himself dumped after she met me at the Citi Field reception. Katie, of course, did the dumping as gently as possible, but Randy was still angry about it, and he still wanted her back.

Which was now impossible.

"Did you say something, Richie?"

By which I think he meant, did I say something mean or upsetting to Katie that might have led to her suicide.

"Never anything but that I loved her."

Which was true.

Maybe I wasn't the best boyfriend, but we'd never had a single argument. We always had fun together, and we never said anything unpleasant to each other. That's not how Katie was, and it's not how I behave with women. My mother made sure of that. Yes it's true that I never committed to marriage, and yes it's true that I probably took our relationship for granted. But I never did anything to hurt her.

Never.

Randy, as full of himself as always, clearly wasn't satisfied.

"I think you drove her off a cliff, Richie."

The idiot Sykes brothers and all the others who were watching clearly agreed.

I figured it was best to shut up and leave.

To extricate myself.

"I'm sorry that you're suffering, Randy, but I need to get going."

"Of course, you do! You're always running away. You're nothing but a dirt-digging sports whore!"

Maybe I was.

Randy was far more reputable, of course. Far more family-friendly. And much more admired by Katie's parents. After all, he was currently at NJ Medical School in Newark.

As I tried to pass by, Randy hit me in the face. Hard. He hit me on the left side of my face, on the patch over my dead eye, and I later wondered if he did it on purpose. It was a powerful sucker punch, and

I was the sucker, but I didn't go down. Instead, I threw a wild punch myself, then grabbed him as we fell to the ground with me on top.

To be honest, I'm not much of a fighter. My last fight was in high school, and I lost pretty badly, but now I was somehow on top of things, so the Sykes brothers quickly pulled me off, and we were separated.

I was grateful.

I had no intention of trying to hit Randy again. Yeah, he was a jerk, but he was a suffering jerk, just like me.

Eventually, Mr. Kovacs appeared in the midst of things.

He wasn't happy.

He sized things up immediately and reprimanded everyone.

"What the hell do you think you're doing?"

No one said a word.

Then he turned and looked at me.

It wasn't hate, it was mostly disappointment.

"You should leave, Richard."

I nodded, the crowd parted, and I exited out into the comfort of the cold December night.

I stared up at the black unforgiving sky, and I spoke directly to God.

Something I seldom do.

"What do you want from me?"

Chapter 11

Saint Peter's Hospital

(Wednesday, 12/15/21)

I was sitting next to the hospital bed.

Next to my dying mother.

Who was unconscious from the morphine and the expectancy of death.

I was distracting myself by reading the old editorials that had changed my life.

"Mr. Wright and Mr. Juice"
"Mr. Commissioner and the Juice Heads"

These were the two screeds about the steroid scandal that my editors had agreed to publish when I was still a twenty-one-year-old intern at the *Newark Star-Ledger*. They certainly took a big risk letting a precocious kid have his say about the intractable PED problem in professional baseball, but it made me famous overnight. (Or as famous as a young unknown sportswriter can get.) Those editorials led to the AAS Award, a full-time position at the *Ledger*, and the attentions of Terry McDonell, the distinguished editor at *Sports Illustrated*, who hired me for selected assignments a few years later.

I'm not really sure why I decided to read them tonight. I hadn't read either of them since they first came out in 2007, over fourteen years ago.

It wasn't a pleasant experience.

I found the young author (me) to be boorish, arrogant, full of himself, self-righteous, and reeking with umbrage.

I didn't care for the kid at all.

Which is not to say that the subject didn't deserve a ton of anger. A ton of umbrage. The MLB steroid scandal, if truth be told, was really a cheating scandal, and far worse than the Black Sox scandal of 1919. For about twenty years, many MLB players were enhancing their abilities with illegal drugs and, as a consequence, cheating the reputable players who kept themselves clean. They were also cheating the fans, and they were also cheating the beautiful game of baseball.

Regarding which Babe Ruth had once said:

Baseball was, is, and always will be to me the best game in the world.

But it was damaged and demeaned by admitted drugies like Mark McGwire, Jose Canseco (read *Juiced*), Jason Giambi, Alex Rodriquez, Ken Caminiti, and Ryan Braun. As well as deceptive deniers like purported Home Run King Barry Bonds, three-hundred-game winner

Roger Clemens, Sammy Sosa, Rafael Palmeiro, Juan Gonzalez, Ivan Rodriquez, and many others. The Mitchell Report, independently overseen by former Senator George Mitchell, named over eighty former and current steroid users in 2007.

Equally devastating was the undeniable fact that while the cheating was happening, Major League Baseball looked the other way. Bud Selig, commissioner from 1998 to 2015, who definitely knew what was going on, was intentionally slow to act. Why rock the boat? Baseball was amazingly popular, home run records were being routinely broken, and the money was pouring in. Who wants a scandal when things are going well? As a result, steroids (which were federally criminalized by the Anti-Drug Abuse Act of 1988) weren't banned from baseball until 2005 and HGH (Human Growth Hormone) wasn't banned until 2011, and even then there was inadequate testing, slap on the wrist fines, and negligible suspensions.

So I guess it's fair to say that the self-important young kid who wrote those two editorials back in 2007 was fully justified in his outrage. As well as justified for calling for the commissioner's resignation. As well as justified for demanding that all drug-enhanced records be invalidated and permanently eliminated from the records books. As well as justified in demanding that the Hall of Fame ban all the steroid cheats.

(Which they seemed to have done so far.)

Oh, well, enough of that.

Enough of young me.

I shut off my phone.

The doctor had told me that my mom probably wouldn't make it through the night, and it was now approaching midnight.

Earlier I'd learned from Lili that Katie's old boyfriend Randy had been questioned by the police, but I found it hard to believe that he could do such a thing. Would he really prefer that Katie was dead rather than be with the likes of me? It was hard to fathom, but Randy was a med student, and he knew a lot more about injections and drugs than I did.

The other primary suspect, of course, was me. I'd also been questioned at length this afternoon, after the morgue and before the funeral parlor. Questioned by two smart rather reticent detectives who held their cards close to their chest. By the time of my interview, I already knew (from a Mack text) that the coroner had placed Katie's time of death around ten o'clock on the night of December 11, when I was sitting ringside at Madison Square Garden watching Lomachenko thump Richard Commey around the ring. Where I'd been seen by numerous witnesses. Regardless, my two Hoboken interrogators (Detectives Smith and Ricardi) wanted a detailed account of my entire evening, so I told them about the Copa and the Philly girls, about my Uber to Sea Girt at the Jersey Shore, and about crashing into my bed half-drunk.

Assiduously, they took notes, then let me go.

I looked down at my mom.

I know it's a cliché to wonder if we've told the people we love that we love them enough, but I believe that I had.

Despite my multitude of other flaws.

My mom was dying fully aware in her heart and soul that her only child, her only son, had loved her unconditionally and that he was unconditionally grateful. She was now sixty years old and had come full circle in her life, ready to die right here in St. Peter's, the very same hospital where she'd been born six decades ago. She'd also been raised right here in New Brunswick by devout Hungarian immigrants. Eventually, after a bio BS and a bio MS at Rutgers, she took a lab tech job at J&J where she met my father.

Lucky him.

Lucky me.

She did her best to raise me as she'd been raised, with love, direction, and encouragement, and, as a result, any subsequent inadequacies that I might have had and still have (which will be assiduously delineated throughout this memorandum) are entirely my own responsibility.

My own failures.

Unlike other people with difficult backgrounds, I have no excuses.

I had marvelous parents.

Then someone interrupted my thoughts.

Someone came into the room.

It wasn't a nurse.

It was Rebeka.

I was surprised.

"How'd you get in here?" I wondered.

"I lied."

"You've never lied in your life."

"I did tonight."

She came over to the bed, looked down at my mom, and gently took her hand.

"Is it tonight, Richie?"

"The doc thinks so."

She pulled up a chair and sat down next to me.

"Don't worry, Richie, I'm not about to cry. I've already cried all the way over here in the car."

Rebeka was my cousin, a maternal cousin and my closest cousin, and she lived right across the Raritan in Highland Park. She was six years younger than me, went to Rutgers for an ED degree, married her boyfriend Jim, a likeable local guy who runs a Heating and AC supply company, while she homeschools their four exemplary kids.

Sometimes she has an unnerving habit of speaking her mind.

"I'm sorry about Katie, Richie. She was a lovely girl, and you should have left her alone and groveled your way back to Cindy."

Yeah, Becky's back in town.

My mom's lying half-dead right next to us, my girlfriend's already dead in a funeral parlor across town, and Rebeka Hancock is reordering my life.

It's true. Rebeka *really did* like Katie. After all, who didn't? But Rebeka was one of Cindy's bridesmaids, and they've remained best friends, even after I was out of the picture. Ever since the divorce, she's been telling me to suck it up, admit that I was wrong (which I was), and try to patch things up.

Before it's too late.

"Why don't we finish burying the dead, Beck?"

She was undaunted. Just like my mom, Becky was a serious Catholic, and death was just a passage to a much better place, especially for the likes of Katie and my mom, so Rebeka was focused on the here and now.

"You'll never get her back if you wait too long," she insisted.

Which seemed rather obvious.

I looked at her directly.

"Why do you think she'd have me again? Do you know something that I don't know."

She shook her head.

A bit frustrated.

"No, moron, Cindy and I talk about everything under the sun, except for you. I never bug her about it. Instead, I bug you."

"Well, bug-off."

She laughed.

I had the feeling that my mom would have laughed too, if she were conscious.

Maybe, in some way, she was.

"By the way, Cindy thinks her stalker is back."

"What! After all this time? Is she sure about it?"

"She's not positive, but it still worries me."

When I didn't say anything, we sat in the silence for a while. Then she stood up abruptly, kissed me on the forehead, then bent over and kissed my mom on her cheek.

"I feel more cries coming on, Richie. So I think I'd better stop down to the chapel before I head back home to my babies."

"Thanks for coming, Beck, and for bossing me around as usual."

"Anytime. We're pals, right?

She smiled her charming smile and left the room.

Leaving me to think about it.

To think about everything.

Rebeka was probably my closest friend, but not really what you'd call a best friend. I guess I really didn't have a best friend, which seems to indicate some kind of inadequacy of character. Sure I had my old New Brunswick pals, and my old Rutgers pals, and even though I was a bit of a maverick in the sports world, I had lots of sportswriter friends and colleagues, but there was no one in particular whom I could call my best friend.

The kind of friend that I could talk to about anything.

The kind of friend who would be sitting right here beside me tonight.

I once read somewhere that only fifty-nine percent of Americans had someone in their life that they considered their best friend. So I guess I wasn't alone.

Becky clearly believed that Cindy was supposed to be my best friend before I blew it.

Maybe she was right.

So I thought some more about Cindy.

Thinking about the first time we met in the stands of a Millville Senior High School baseball game in 2008, when Mike Trout pitched a no-hitter for the Thunderbolts. (Yes, Mike Trout was a pitcher before moving to centerfield.) After one of his impressive strikeouts, she'd excitedly spilled her Cracker Jacks all over me. She was sitting right next to me at the time, and she laughed and smiled, and that was all she wrote! She was nineteen at the time, she was studying Latin at Princeton, which seemed rather ridiculous to me, and we crashed into love. We married the following year, and I crashed the marriage the following year.

As Rebeka would say, I blew it.

For some reason I thought of one of Cindy's favorite songs. She was a south Jersey girl, and she loved country music, especially singers like Pam Tillis, Carlene Carter, Doug Stone, Lorrie Morgan, Kathy Mattea, and Dwight Yoakam. But her most favorite of all was Hal Ketchum (who sadly died last year). I remember driving all around south Jersey with Cindy sitting right next to me and singing along with "Small Town Saturday Night," "Wings of a Dove," "Five O'clock World," and one of Ketchum's own beautiful compositions "I Know Where Love Lives."

Which was the favorite of her favorites.

Love don't hang out in a grand hotel,
Got no satin sheets, got no servant's bell . . .

And the chorus, now softly singing in my head.

I know where love lives,
She's sitting on the back step in the evening air,
Sea-green eyes and her chestnut hair.

Then the memory faded.
Then ended.

I took my mom's unresponsive hand.
And waited.

Chapter 12

St. Ladislaus

(Saturday, 12/18/21)

G ently:

In Paradisum deducant te Angeli . . . .

Exactly.

May the angels lead you into Paradise . . . .

I was back at St. Ladislaus.

This time I was sitting up front.

In the first pew.

Two days ago for Katie's funeral, I sat in the back and left before the final blessing. My presence had already caused enough of a commotion at the wake, and even though her family and friends would now be aware that someone else (possibly Randy Pierce) had murdered their beloved Katie, I still had the feeling that I was persona non grata. So I did my best to be invisible and decided not to attend the burial at Resurrection Cemetery in nearby Piscataway.

Now it was my mother's turn.

Father Nagy had been very busy the past few days, offering two traditional requiem Masses for two women from different generations who were very much admired in the parish.

Rebeka sat beside me, along with her husband Jim and the five kids. Just like two days ago, the church was packed. My mom had many close friends within the parish, as well as many close friends at J&J.

Dr. K. and her family were sitting right behind me.

Together, we all prayed for the dead.

That God would forgive her her trespasses.

Which were few and far between.

Catholics are very adept at praying for the dead, even though it's a notion that some believe is pointless and fruitless. When I was a kid at my grandfather's funeral, I wondered about it myself, so later that night when we got back home I asked my mother about it.

That was back when I was still curious about things not covered on the sports page.

"It's tied up with the notion of purgatory," she explained, "and the communion of saints. You should know that, Richie."

I did know it, at least as well as a twelve-year-old could apprehend such things.

"Is it in the Bible?" I wondered.

She laughed.

"So who's the new theologian in town!"

I laughed too, and figured that it was over, but I'd unfortunately opened up the door.

"In Maccabees II, the last book of the Old Testament," she explained, "Judas and his men pray for their dead comrades after victory in battle."

"Judas?"

"Not that Judas! Judas Maccabeus who led the Jewish revolt against the Seleucids."

Which helped.

A little.

She wasn't done.

"In St. Paul's letter to Timothy, he prays for the deceased Onesiphorus."

She could see that I was bored to death.

"I can see," she kidded, "that you'd like to hear even more."

When I said nothing, she laughed and continued.

"Praying for the dead was confirmed in the writings of Tertullian, Cyprian, Ambrose, Augustine, Chrysostom, and others that I can't remember. It was also instructed in numerous inscriptions in the Roman Catacombs."

Once again, I said nothing.

"Aren't you glad you asked?"

"Not really, Mom."

"Fine, now go and say a few prayers for your grandfather."

Which I did.

It was the last religious question I ever asked her, but it was definitely not the last religious instruction that I ever received from my mom.

Now she was dead herself, and I was praying for her.

Not that I believed she really needed it, but as she also told me one other time, "Sincere prayers never go to waste."

So I was thinking about my mom, but I was also distracted by someone else.

Cindy had shown up in New Brunswick to pay her respects. I'd seen her arrive just before Mass, and she looked just as lovely as always.

She came right up to me and took my hands in hers.

"I'm so sorry, Richard. It was impossible not to love your mom."

Then she kissed me on the cheek, entered the back of the church with her sister Melanie, and I never saw her again.

But I knew she was back there somewhere.

Somewhere behind me.

After Mass, I looked around, but she was gone.

After the burial at Resurrection, I came back to St. Ladislaus and waited for Fr. Nagy in the back of the church.

As previously arranged.

My cell vibrated.

It was Mack.

Rohypnol in the prelim tox report. Lots.

No surprise.

Whoever killed Katie had certainly incapacitated her before the lethal injection, and I knew enough about Rohypnol to assume that it could effectively knock her out.

Eventually, the old priest came out of the sacristy and made his way to the back of his church.

Fr. Kristof Nagy was my mother's confessor. He was born in Szolnok and escaped Communist Hungary with his family when he was ten years old during the failed revolt in 1956. His family found welcoming comfort within the Hungarian community in New Brunswick, and he eventually became a diocesan priest and served his entire priestly life here at St. Ladislaus. These days, he was somewhere in his mid-seventies, and he'd once been the pastor at Ladislaus, but now he was perfectly content to serve as pastor emeritus.

I'd always liked him, but I was never as close to him as my parents were. Or as Katie was. The man was kind and earnest with a sense of humor. He was also a baseball fan.

A Mets fan.

"I hope things went well today," he said.

"Perfect, Father. My mom would have been perfectly pleased."

Given that, he was clearly uncertain why I'd asked to meet with him.

"Should we talk here or in the rectory?"

"This is fine."

He nodded, then sat down beside me.

"What is it, Richard?"

I wasn't exactly sure.

"It's hard to explain."

"Is it related to your mother's death? Or Katie's?"

"Not really. It's been going on for a long time."

"What?"

I shrugged.

"I'm not happy with myself."

Which sounded embarrassingly pathetic to me, but the priest, who'd surely been hearing stuff like this all throughout his entire priestly life, waited patiently.

Maybe it wasn't all that hard to explain.

I got right to it.

"I feel that my life is frivolous."

Just for the hell of it, I'd looked up the word earlier today.

of little weight or importance
lacking in seriousness

It had even far more disturbing synonyms.

silly
trivial

"I don't understand," he said.

I tried to clarify.

"I feel as though nothing that I do has any real consequence."

"Many people question what they're doing with their lives, Richard."

"But is there anything more worthless than writing about games and sports."

I could tell that he was taken aback by the idea, so I tried to explain myself better.

"I'm not an especially good Catholic, Father, but I know that we're accountable for what we do with our lives, and I also believe that one's life is a gift, and that the time we're given is also a gift. So what do I do with mine? I write about essentially meaningless activities. Let's face it, nothing that I write will have any consequence or significance in a hundred years. Or fifty years. Or even ten years."

It didn't feel like I was whining, but maybe I was. This problem, which seemed intractable, was deadly serious to me, and I was glad to see that it also seemed serious to the old priest.

After all, what the hell *are* we supposed to do with our lives?

"But sports gives people pleasure, Richie. I keep up with the Mets every day during the season, and I appreciate all the news and analysis."

"Yes, and there's nothing wrong with some entertainment in our lives, but for me it's not just entertainment, it's *everything*. Almost every waking hour of the past fourteen years of my life has been nothing else. Nothing but games and more games. How can that be a justifiable life?"

"But many people probably feel that they lead lives without consequence. Right? What about the factory worker or the clerk in the mall or the bank teller?"

"But they're all, assuming they're honest, doing some good in this world. Making products, selling products, helping people manage their money, etc. I produce absolutely nothing meaningful, and I help no one, except for maybe providing a bit of frivolous entertainment."

"But you're making a living, Richie. You're supporting yourself."

"So is the mobster. So is the pornographer. I'm not saying that what I'm doing is entirely morally bankrupt, but sometimes I feel as if my life itself is morally bankrupt."

He went silent.

Thoughtfully.

"Can I quote someone?" I asked.

"Of course, who do you have in mind?"

"Ken Griffey Jr."

He smiled.

"Tell me."

So I did.

It was something (like the Jimmy Cannon quote about the "toy department of life") that had been bugging me for a long time.

Baseball is not a life-or-death situation, and in the big picture, this game is just a small part of our lives. The important thing is to use baseball to help other people.

As Fr. Nagy nodded, thinking it over, I felt that I should clarify something.

"Don't worry, Father, I'm not about to jump off the GW Bridge, and I'm not even depressive about it. I suppose I'm too self-satisfied to be depressed. But I'm definitely concerned about it. I'm thirty-five-years-old, Father. Am I supposed to spend the rest of my life talking about sports. About games? Aren't I accountable for what I do with my life."

"Of course, we all are."

Then he stood up, which surprised me.

"Let me think about it, Richard."

I stood up as well.

"I'd appreciate it, Father. Maybe I'm just being self-absorbed."

"Maybe not."

We shook hands, and he walked down the main aisle, genuflected at the altar, and went into the sacristy.

I suppose I'd just made a fool of myself.

Maybe not.

Chapter 13

Covid

(Thursday, 12/23/21)

Yeah, I got it.

But not too bad.

Some initial fever, some coughing, but mostly feeling terribly, lousy, like crap. Feeling like I had the flu.

It started four days ago and things had been improving. I certainly wasn't about to complain about it given that Covid-19 had been a pandemic killer. Ever since it had arrived from China in 2019, there'd been over three hundred million cases worldwide with four million dead, including about a million in the US.

Increasing every day.

Yeah, I got my shots. Both Pfizers. And I'd worn my mask everywhere I was supposed to wear it, even though I'm not convinced that it did much good. Regardless, despite getting knocked out for a few days, I was one of the lucky ones who wasn't in any of the high-risk categories: over sixty-five, overweight, diabetes, heart and lung issues, smokers, etc.

Since I was feeling a bit better today, I tried to occupy my muddled mind by watching *Jerry McGuire*, which was one of my favorites.

I've never been a big film or TV watcher (excepting for sporting events of course), which always amused Simon Gerard, my film critic pal.

"*Everyone* watches films, Richard!" he'd pontificate, "Every American watches at least fifteen films a month. One every other day! And that doesn't even count television. What the hell's the matter with you?"

Even though I had some serious doubts about his statistics, I let it go. He was obviously having fun.

"I'm too busy," I said stupidly.

"Yeah, sure, Richie, sports, sports, sports!"

"What about you, Simon? Films, films, films."

He nodded a bit and thought it over.

"Yeah, you're right about that," he admitted, but he wasn't letting me off the hook.

"Well, what about sports films, Richie? Surely, you've watched a ton of them."

"Not really. Just *Rocky* and *Pride of the Yankees*."

"That's it?" he said incredulously.

"That's it."

So he gave me a long list to watch.

"And when you're finished," he added, "I want to hear your top five."

"Fine."

I can't remember all the titles but the list included *Hoosiers, Field of Dreams, Miracle, Friday Night Lights, Bull Durham, White Men Can't Jump, Eight Men Out, 42, The Color of Money, The Natural, Secretariat, The Fighter, We are Marshall, The Hustler, Remember the Titans, Raging Bull, Invictus, The Blind Side, Cinderella Man*, and a bunch more.

So I watched a film every week for about three months. I figured that a sportswriter like myself should probably be familiar with the more famous sports films, which other writers often referenced in their columns and articles.

I'll admit that I did enjoy some of them, but I also didn't enjoy some of them, and the rest were somewhere in the middle. Take them or leave them. Give me a ballgame any day of the week.

But I did my due diligence, and I texted Simon the results.

Jerry McGuire
Rocky
Chariots of Fire
Moneyball

He texted right back.

That's only four.

Me:

I'm sticking with four.

Simon:

What about Field of Dreams *or* The Natural *or any of the other baseball flicks? I'm shocked!*

I called him immediately and explained that I thought *The Natural* and *Dreams* were way too arty and not realistic enough.

"You're an idiot," he decided.

Maybe I was.

But I did like *Jerry McGuire.* Maybe because the guy was a jerk like me, and he actually did something about it. One day, he unexpectedly "grew a conscience," and he had an epiphany and then a breakthrough. Or was it a breakdown? Or both? As for me, I very much liked his "mission statement," and I liked his honest self-admission.

I hated myself. No, no, no. Here's what it was – I hated my place in the world.

I also liked the film's romance, the performances, the dialogue, and how it portrayed the ruthless side of sports agenting.

Yes, I *really* did enjoy the romance, and how Jerry managed to salvage his marriage. How he told her that he loved her in a room crowded with divorced women, and how she said, "You had me at 'Hello.'"

Jerry McGuire was just some character in a movie, but he was still a better man than me. I'd wrecked my marriage, and I'd apparently impregnated another man's wife.

I disgusted myself.

As for the pregnancy and the resultant child, Irene still hadn't responded to my text eleven days ago after she dropped her bombshell, and I'd responded:

Are you sure?

Since then I'd called, emailed, and texted.

Nothing.

Now I was fed up, and I was feeling lousy anyway, so I called her again, and I left another message.

Look, Irene. I'm coming down there to pound on your front door if you don't respond.

Fifteen minutes later, my cell hummed.

A text.

Sorry, Richie, it was all a lie. I was lonely and drunk and Ben was off at some stupid medical conference. Please forgive me.

Which seemed suspicious given that she really didn't like her husband very much. But maybe she'd been lying about that too.

I texted right back.

Is the boy mine or not?

Her response was immediate.

Of course not!

I was disgusted, but it felt good to be disgusted with someone other than myself.

My cell phone rang.

I picked up.

It was Mack, who usually texts.

"I wanted to let you know that they've arrested Randall Peirce."

"Do they have anything?"

"I don't know, but the guy doesn't seem to have a good alibi. It's one of those 'I was home alone watching television' alibis. Which isn't very convincing, especially for a young guy on a Saturday night."

"Maybe, maybe not."

"But that's not the real reason I'm calling."

I waited.

"Have you seen the podcast?"

"What podcast?"

Chapter 14

Podcast

(Thursday, 12/23/21)

Zabrina always talks too much.

She's also too damned honest and too damned earnest.

As always, she was looking great. She was sporting a dark-green blazer with a light-green blouse, both of which highlighted her soft green eyes and her dirty blonde cropped hair. At the moment, she was sitting with Eden Steele on Eden's YouTube podcast, *Sportswomen*, which was a rerun of a show that had aired earlier tonight.

As soon as Mack warned me about it, I shut off my phone, and went looking for the podcast on my laptop. I knew what was coming, but I hoped that it wouldn't be as bad as it could be.

It was worse.

The *Sportswomen* podcast focuses on the role of female athletes in their profession and society at large. It's especially concerned about how women athletes are treated by employers, coaches, sponsors, and the media – concerned about all the difficulties that women athletes face day in and day out.

It was a subject that Zabrina certainly knew a lot about. For the past five years, she'd been covering the WNBA, especially the New York Liberty, for the *Daily News*, and she was very well-connected and respected across the industry. I'd always done my best to help her in her career, and when she wanted to meet at Jack Doyle's twelve days ago before the Lomachenko-Commey fight at the Garden, I went along with the idea because I assumed that she needed help of some kind.

I was wrong.

She rambled on and on about how women aren't always treated fairly in the sports world, which was definitely accurate, but which I couldn't do anything about over a steak at Jack Doyle's. Instead, I remember sitting there thinking about my girlfriend across the Hudson.

The one who wanted to marry me.

The one who would die later the same night.

At present, I pushed it all from my mind and focused on the show.

Needless to say, tonight's *Sportswomen* podcast was concerned about the same problems, about the mental, physical, and sexual harassment and abuse that can happen in the world of sports. The specific topic for the episode was the effects of the Me Too Movement on the sporting world, and the subsequent changes in legislation in various states regarding the statute of limitations.

In the past in New Jersey, victims of sexual assault and/or rape had two years to press charges against their offenders, but earlier this year the state legislature, with the governor's signature, passed S477/A3648 which essentially eliminated the statute of limitations for sexual assault.

Both Zabrina and Eden had been strong proponents of the bill (so was I), and both had testified during the preliminary hearings last year.

Eden: So, Zabrina, are you satisfied with S477?

Zabrina: I am, Eden. Now women who were hesitant to come forward in the past, and who only had a narrow window to seek justice, can accuse the criminals publicly – and hopefully get some kind of justice.

Eden: We've seen what happened in Hollywood with the Weinstein case, and we've also seen the convictions of Larry Nasser who horribly abused countless young gymnasts at Michigan State. Do you think, in the wake of S477, there will be other cases surfacing in the sports world?

Zabrina: I hope so, Eden. I know of at least one case myself that took place in Hoboken ten years ago at a sportswriter's condo which I hope will finally come to light.

[Eden, unsurprisingly, looked a bit shocked.]

Eden: Can you tell us anything about it?

Zabrina: Well, it's not really my place, Eden. It's up to the victim.

Eden: Is there any evidence?

Zabrina: Yes, there is, and a witness as well.

[Eden looked stunned.]

Zabrina (continuing): But that's all I can say about it right now, Eden. I'm sure you understand.

Eden nodded, and I paused the telecast, as I sat on my Covid couch and remembered everything.

After all, *I* was the witness!

Years ago, when I first broke into the business at the *Star-Ledger*, Gordon Calhoun, known to everyone as "Cal," was one of the senior reporters on the staff, and he generously took me under his wing. As a sportswriter, he was always clear, concise, and uncontroversial on a variety of sports. Mostly he covered the Mets and the Jets, but he also had a lifelong interest in the trotters and golf. He was quite an entertaining storyteller, who definitely liked his beer way too much, but was generally liked by everyone. He was especially helpful to young writers like myself, as well as various young athletes from around the Garden State.

So Cal became my mentor and my friend, and it was Cal who convinced the paper's editors to allow me to write the editorial ("Mr. Wright and Mr. Juice") that kickstarted my career with a bang when I was only twenty-one years old. It would be fair to say that I owe a lot to Cal Calhoun.

If not everything.

Once the money started rolling in, I bought a rather upscale condo on the Waterfront in Hoboken, not far from Sinatra Park. The views of Manhattan were astonishing, the nightlife was the best in New Jersey, and I was a regular at the House of Que (barbeque), Grimaldi's Pizzeria, Carlo's Bakery, and Moran's Pub. At the time, I was still covering the Mets, as well as a young high school phenom in south Jersey named Michael Trout. My life was lively, fast, easy, and sometimes over-indulgent.

I was young and full of myself.

Then things got even better.

Sports Illustrated came knocking, and I met and married Cindy.

But a year later our marriage fell apart, and we were soon divorced. Alone again, I divided my time between my condo in Hoboken, which no longer seemed all that attractive, and my parents' isolated cottage down at the New Jersey shore.

As for Cal, his life was heading in the same direction. His writings had gone stale, even routine, he was now thrice divorced, and he was drinking far too many Coronas. Sometimes, even though I didn't see him very much anymore, I'd let him crash at my condo in Hoboken, where I assumed he was sleeping off too much booze.

Nevertheless, he was still helping young athletes.

One of whom was a young golfing star at Princeton from Moorestown named Angie Anderson, who was ranked third in the NCAA national standings during her senior year and who seemed a likely prospect for the WPGA.

Then it happened.

Ten years ago.

I was in Manhattan that night for a Miguel Cotto fight at the Garden. He lost. After some post-fight drinks at Crompton's in Chelsea, I Ubered back to Hoboken rather than going all the way down to the shore. When I arrived at the front door of my condo, I could hear some commotion inside. Naturally, I figured that Cal was drunk and knocking some stuff around, and I remember thinking, "I hope that old bastard hasn't smash my AAS award," but, of course, it was much worse than that.

I heard some moans.

I also heard a weak, "No."

I also heard a weak, "Stop."

Immediately, I followed the noises into my guest room, and Cal was obviously raping a young woman on top of the bed. She'd clearly been smashed in the mouth, and her face was bleeding. Her clothes were still on but partly torn away. She was crying and helpless. Cal Calhoun was well over two hundred pounds and strong like an ex-linebacker.

Which he'd been in high school.

For some reason, despite the shock of it all, I didn't hesitate. I pulled Cal off the girl and smashed him hard into the wall next to the bed. Concussed as well as drunk, he fell unconscious to the floor.

I looked down at the young woman.

I'd never met her before, but I'd seen her in golf photographs and videos, and I knew that it was Angie Anderson.

But I didn't know what I should do.

Eventually, I helped her sit up on the edge of the bed. She covered herself as well as she could, and she wiped some of the dripping blood from her face.

"Thank you," she said softly.

"I'm calling the police," I said.

But when I took out my phone, she reached over and prevented me from dialing 911.

"Please don't."

That's all she said.

So I waited, hoping that she'd change her mind.

"Are you sure?"

"I am."

"What can I do?"

"Could you drive me back to Princeton?"

"Are you sure about this, Angie?" I tried again.

"Yes."

She stood up unsteadily, walked into the bathroom, washed herself off, and I drove her back to her dorm at Princeton.

Mostly in silence.

But she did make it perfectly clear why she'd been in Hoboken.

"He told me that you were having a party, and that he wanted to introduce me to David Winkle."

Winkle was a top golf agent at Hambric Sports, which represented Scottie Scheffler and many other big-name golfers.

"There was never," she added, "anything romantic between us. *Never.*"

Of which I had no doubt. She was eighteen years old back then, and Cal was a worn-out fifty-five.

After I dropped her off at her dorm that night, I never saw her again.

A few days later I sent her a text:

I hope you're doing ok, Angie. Let me know if there's anything I can do.

She responded:

Thank you, Richard. For everything.

It was perfectly clear that she wanted to try and forget about what had happened. It was equally clear that she didn't want to be plastered all over the web as a "victim."

When I drove back to Hoboken from Princeton that night, I was astonished to discover that Cal was still in my condo, sitting on the couch in my living room. I was furious, which is an emotion that I don't often feel, and I was ready to physically throw him out the front door.

Then I saw the gun.

I don't know what kind it was, but the barrel was pointing upward under his chin.

I didn't even know he had a gun.

Why?

What for?

The guy was a total mess. His face was badly bruised where he'd hit the bedroom wall, and his eyes were wet and weary with self-disgust.

But I had no sympathy.

Rapists, as far as I'm concerned, should be publicly hung from the gallows in the village square. If the bastard was determined to kill himself, it was fine with me.

Then I said what I surely shouldn't have said.

"Go ahead, asshole."

Meaning pull the trigger.

He looked at me blankly, but he was definitely thinking about it.

Then he lowered the gun to his lap. He couldn't go through with it.

I opened the front door.

"Get the hell out, Cal!" I threatened him.

He rose unsteadily from the couch, staggered through the front door, and I slammed it behind him.

Then Zabrina called.

Did I mention that Zabrina and Angie were not only close friends but dormmates at Princeton?

I picked it up.

"How is she?" I asked.

"Devastated. She took a shower, and I got her to bed, and she's sleeping now."

"I tried to call it in."

"I know. She told me. She just wants it to go away."

"Maybe she'll change her mind."

"Maybe, maybe not."

There was silence on the line.

"I've done what maybe I had no right to do," she admitted.

I waited.

"I pulled back the covers when she fell asleep and took some pictures of her bruises. I've also put her panties in a plastic bag in case she ever changes her mind. Have I gone too far, Richie?"

"I think you've done exactly the right thing, but it's up to her. If she wants to go after him, she's got two witnesses, photos, and DNA."

"I still feel lousy about it."

"Don't."

That was that.

I also felt lousy about it. Worse than lousy.

Did I do the right thing?

(What would *you* do?)

Let's face it, I'd let a criminal walk, and it would bother me for the next ten years.

As for Angie, she never told the police what happened that night, and according to Zabrina, it changed her quite a bit. Which was perfectly understandable. She grew more cautious, and she grew less ambitious, especially regarding her career and the WPGA tour. She preferred staying close to her family in Moorestown. She was still an excellent golfer, and through her Jersey and Princeton connections, she secured a position as a course pro at Pine Valley, one of the best golf courses in New Jersey, created by George Crump in the sandy Pine Barrens of southwest NJ.

Now Zabrina was on the web talking about it.

A bit too freely.

Even mentioning a sportswriter's condo in Hoboken.

I wondered how long it would take the press to zone in on me.

As a suspect!

I turned on my phone. There were a million texts, a million phone messages, and a million emails.

It was just before midnight.

I was screwed and I knew it.

They'd be banging on my door any minute, and I needed to get out of Dodge.

Lingering Covid or not.

I needed to pack a bag quickly, drive down to Sea Girt, and hide myself as best I could.

Then another thought occurred to me.

An ugly thought.

After that night in Hoboken, Cal, expecting the worst, resigned from the *Star-Ledger* and immediately moved out of state. I never saw him again, but he did send me a text a few days after the rape.

I'm sorry, Richie. I could really use a friend right now.

Screw him.

I never texted him back.

That was ten years ago.

Maybe he hated me for what I did that night. For smashing his face and encouraging him to blow his brains out. Then cutting him off entirely. Maybe he'd spent the past ten years hating me. Maybe he'd wanted to get back at me. Maybe he'd killed my Katie!

I know it seems far-fetched, but during the last twelve days, *everything* in my life had seemed far-fetched.

I stood up, packed a small bag, and took 95 over to the Parkway.

Then down to the ocean.

Chapter 15

Sea Girt

(Friday, 12/24/21)

Christmas Eve.

I was staring at the ocean again.

It was dark and turbulent beneath an overcast December sky. Ominous, dangerous, beautiful. For some reason, I thought of Hebrews 9:27, which some radio evangelist had been talking about last night as I was searching through the FM channels on my drive down the Parkway to Sea Girt.

As it is appointed for men once to die, and after this the judgment.

I immediately changed the station. I certainly didn't want to hear some random guy's explication about St. Paul's theological meanings. After all, it was pretty obvious. We'll all end up dead, and we'll all be held accountable.

As for me, I wasn't feeling very "accountable" these days.

My phone, of course, was still blowing up, but fortunately the press hadn't shown up at my front door. Not yet. Only a few family and friends knew about my Sea Girt cottage, but reporters are relentless (I should know), and I wondered if I'd soon need to move to a hotel somewhere. Maybe out of state.

I wasn't really feeling sorry for myself, just confused. I didn't know what I was supposed to do. Or what I was supposed to say. I had no idea what was the morally right thing to do, and I wished more than anything that I could talk to my mother about it. Or my father. But I was on my own.

Maybe I should talk to a priest?

A seemingly lost seagull fluttered across the ocean's rough surface through the chilling breeze. I wondered how Angie Anderson was doing. The press had already assumed that she was the young woman who was raped by someone (me?) in my condo ten years ago in Hoboken, and I'm sure that she and her family in Moorestown were under a relentless siege.

So far she'd said nothing about any of it.

Zabrina had also dropped off the face of the earth. She'd been a perfect idiot last night on the podcast, having exposed her close friend. But despite her stupidity, I felt sorry for her as well.

I pushed it out of my mind.

Earlier this morning, to distract myself, I watched *Frequency* again. For probably the tenth time. When I told Simon a few years ago that it was now my favorite sports film (becoming the missing fifth film in my "top five" list), he dismissed the idea out of hand, rightly pointing out that it's really a crime thriller with a bit of sci-fi hocus-pocus thrown in. If you've never seen it, it takes place during a weird aurora borealis over New York City in 1999 when a young cop (Jim Caviezel) discovers his dead father's old Heathkit ham radio. When he plugs it in, he somehow makes audio contact with his father (Dennis Quaid) back in 1969 (thirty years earlier!) during the famous World Series when the Amazing Mets beat the heavily favored Baltimore Orioles. The baseball theme is just an enjoyable backstory in the film but the son's knowledge of what will happen in the series (including the famous Cleon Jones "shoe polish incident" in Game 5) helps to identify the serial killer.

It's all a bit complicated, and I'm not sure that I fully follow it all, but it ends up happily, and I've always enjoyed it.

Even earlier today.

It made me think of the first time I watched it, at Katie's insistence, when we were first dating in 2018 after we'd met at the reception at Citi Field for my new book *Amazin'*. Given that Katie was a lifetime Mets fan who worked in the team's PR office, she naturally loved the film, and we watched it together and discussed it for hours over a bottle and a half of Merlot.

Eventually, inevitably, she asked me about the stacks of baseball quotes that I was collecting for *Quips: Sports Quotes*, the proposed follow-up to my successful *Nicks: Sports Nicknames*.

"What's your all-time favorite baseball quote?" she asked.

"That's easy, Katie. It's what Leo Durocher said when he first saw Willie Mays approaching after Willie had been called up to the New York Giants in 1951 after batting .477 in the minors."

Here comes the pennant!

Katie laughed, then she asked for more.

[As have you.]

The greatest baseball players of all-time:

Babe Ruth

Willie Mays

Walter Johnson

[With respects to Cobb, Wagner, Josh Gibson, Musial, Williams, Aaron, Trout and Ohtani]

Classic quotes:

It's a beautiful day for a ballgame. Let's play two! (Ernie Banks)

It' ain't over till it's over. (Yogi Berra)

Yet today I consider myself to be the luckiest man on the face of the earth. (Lou Gehrig)

Nice guys finish last. (Leo Durocher)

Wait till next year. (Brooklyn Dodger fans)

Baseball was, is, and always will be to me the best game in the world. (Babe Ruth)

There are only two seasons – winter and baseball. (Bill Veeck)

Personal favorites:

His fastball looked about the size of a watermelon seed and it hissed at you as it passed. (Ty Cobb on Walter Johnson)

Whoever would understand the heart and mind of America had better learn baseball. (Jacques Barzun)

There have been only two geniuses in the world: Willie Mays and Willie Shakespeare. (Tallulah Bankhead)

Only boring people find baseball boring. (Peter Golenbock)

Washington: First in war, first in peace, and last in the American League. (Charles Dryden)

Next to religion, baseball has had a greater impact on the American people than any other institution. (Herbert Hoover)

They throw the ball, I hit it. They hit the ball, I catch it. (Willie Mays)

I looked out at the Atlantic and thanked God for baseball. It was always capable of distracting me from the unpleasantnesses of life. Unfortunately, I also used it to distract myself from all my personal failings.

All my sins.

Then I heard Katie from behind me.

Softly.

"Richie."

I turned around.

It wasn't Katie, of course, but it was another surprise walking toward me across the hard grey winter sand.

It was the woman that the press was searching for.

Angie Anderson, now twenty-eight years old, still lovely, wearing a bright red mackintosh against the ocean breeze.

As usual, I didn't know what to do, so I stood there like an idiot.

"Angie," I said stupidly.

She came right up to me and hugged me close.

All awkwardness was immediately dispelled.

She let me go, and she looked out at the black ocean.

"Looking for answers?" she asked.

"Yes."

"Any luck?"

"None. What about you?"

She looked back at the cottage.

"Maybe we should go inside," she said evasively.

"Of course."

We entered my parents' beach house through the back door, kicked off our sandy shoes, and went right into the living room.

I gestured at the couch, and she sat down.

"Do you want anything, Angie? Coffee? Hot chocolate?"

"I'm good, Richie."

She looked around the room.

"It's lovely here."

She was right. I've always taken the place for granted. The wooden walls, the winter seascapes, the mahogany bookcases, the small stone fireplace, the comfortable furniture, the perfect lighting fixtures. Very homey, very cozy.

"It was all my mom," I explained.

Angie smiled.

"Well, I didn't think for a minute that it was you!"

She seemed in much better spirits than I would have expected.

"It's nice to see you smile," I said.

"I think the drive from Moorestown did me some good, but I'm not sure that you'll be happy to hear what I have to say."

"Just say it, Angie. I'm ready to do whatever you want me to do."

"I want you to lie, Richie, because I'm planning to deny everything. I'm planning to send out a press release later today categorically denying that the rape victim whom Zabrina alluded to last night was me."

When I didn't say anything, she elaborated further.

"I just can't deal with this right now, Richie, and I want it all to go away. To blow over. I plan to deny that I ever went to Hoboken that night and deny that you and I have ever met. Can you go along with that?"

"Of course."

I didn't know if it was right or wrong (even though lying is obviously wrong), but I was willing to help her in any way that I was capable.

To protect her.

To shelter her.

Greatly relieved and overcome, she cried.

Deeply.

All her smiles were gone.

Unsure what I should do, I went over to the couch, sat down beside her, and held her hand until it was over.

Nothing more needed to be said.

She stood up to leave, and I walked her out the front door to her green Taurus and held open the driver's side door.

"God bless you, Angie," I said, surprising myself. Normally it would have sounded perfectly hypocritical coming from the likes of me, but today I really meant it.

Please, dear God, help this struggling woman.

She kissed me on the cheek.

"I can never thank you enough."

Then she got into her car and drove away, leaving me just as screwed up as I was before she arrived.

Maybe worse.

Just a few hours away from a parentless Christmas.

Just a few hours away from a girlfriendless Christmas.

Chapter 16

Christmas Eve

(Friday, 12/24/21)

Even reporters take a break at Christmas.

Right?

There was a knock at my door.

I was trying to film-distract myself once again. I was watching *It's a Wonderful Life*, which my parents and I watched every Christmas after morning Mass. Which is very hopeful and inspiring, right? Family man George Bailey (Jimmy Stewart) is down and out and suicidal in Bedford Falls, New York (which was apparently based on Califon, New Jersey, which is about seventy-five miles northwest of Sea Girt, which is exactly the kind of factoid my parents were fond of citing on Christmases past). But so many people in the town are praying for George that a most unlikely angel named Clarence is sent to intervene. Regardless, George is still distraught, admitting, "I suppose it would have been better if I'd never been born at all." Clarence is naturally horrified by the notion and decides to show George how his family and friends and community would have suffered if he'd never existed.

The director Frank Capra once said that the film was intended to be an alternative to the "modern trend of atheism" (another parental factoid), and it's become one of the most popular films of all time. With both believers and non-believers alike. Because it shows the inherent worth in the life of an individual. But the problem (at least it's my problem at the age of thirty-five) is that George Bailey was a fundamentally good person who was both self-sacrificing and generous. He was a decent man who really did affect the lives of those around him. So it was fair for me to ask myself: What had I really done in my life that had made the world a better place?

The Ken Griffey quote surfaced again in my brain.

Baseball is not a life-or-death situation, and in the big picture, this game is just a small part of our lives. The important thing is to use baseball to help other people.

Yeah I suppose I've helped a few young sportswriters, and yeah I have some friends who like me, but I'd totally wrecked my marriage, I was apparently insensitive to my girlfriend, and I might (or might not) have gotten another man's wife pregnant.

I know this all sounds rather maudlin and self-pitying, but I wasn't really feeling that sorry for myself. It was more of an objective and clinical reevaluation. I was asking myself, as I'd done numerous times recently, not only what *have* I done with my life, but what *am* I doing with my life.

George Bailey had saved his younger brother's life when they were skating one day. As for me, I've written a bunch of inconsequential sports reports and sports opinions.

Confronted with that uncomfortable thought, I retreated, as always, into the universe of sports to ignore whatever was difficult. I've always been a speed-skating enthusiast, and I remember that the greatest of them all, Eric Heiden (five gold medals back in 1980) had once said.

I really liked it best when I was a nobody.

Which was appropriately humble for an Olympic champ who later when on to become a renowned orthopedic surgeon.

To help people.

So I ran another quote through my mind. This one from the legendary speedskater Bonnie Blair (also five Olympic golds) on her retirement.

I'm definitely going to miss hearing the sound of that gun.

Meaning the starting pistol.

Which always made me smile.

Then there was that knock on my door.

So much for smiles.

I shut off the television and went to the door, thinking about how I needed to pack once again and hide out at some hotel until Angie's press release was finally released.

I opened the front door, determined to be congenial.

To be diplomatic.

It was Cal.

I hadn't seen him in ten years, ever since that hellacious night in Hoboken. He looked like hell. He looked like one of the characters in the dive bar in Pottersville, the sleazy town conjured up by Clarence to show George Baily the tragic fate of some of his friends and neighbors.

He was disheveled, twenty pounds heavier, with a sorry-looking grey beard. Even his clothes looked worn out and neglected.

He was also drunk.

I could smell the Coronas on the evening's dead cold December air.

I said nothing.

"Can I come in?" he tried weakly.

"No, Cal," I said firmly, "I want nothing to do with you."

I really wanted to tell him to drive to the Hoboken police department and confess what he'd done, but, of course, that's not what Angie wanted.

"Please, Richie," he said pathetically. "I need someone to talk to."

"You need a priest," I said, fully aware that he wasn't the only one in Sea Girt who needed some spiritual guidance.

Frustrated, he gave up. He turned around and started walking towards his Ford Fusion.

I couldn't resist.

"How many others were there, Cal?" I called out.

He turned and looked at me coldly.

Then he sneered out a very popular New Jersey two-word expletive ending with the word "you."

Then he slumped down in his car and drove off to God-knows-where.

Did I really want to know if there were others? I'm not sure. Hopefully, it was just a one-time aberration, but I had my doubts. So I tried not to think about it, especially given the fact that he was, once again, going to get away with it.

I shut the front door.

Was I too hard?

Was I too uncharitable?

Was I too unChristian?

Maybe I was, but after seeing Angie earlier today, I felt fine with sending him packing.

Screw him.

Screw Cal.

I sat on my couch and stared at one of my mom's winter seascapes that mimicked the December ocean right outside the cottage.

I had a lot to think about.

Chapter 17

Midnight Mass

(Saturday, 12/25/21)

Why not?

I drove up to St. Ladislaus, and I sat in the back of the church to avoid running into any of my mom's friends. I also stayed in my pew during Communion, feeling myself unworthy. Regardless, everything around me was quite beautiful. The old church was festive with red poinsettias and the golden glow of a million soft warm candles. *Christus Natus Est!* There were also a few select and much appreciated Hungarian references in Fr. Nagy's sermon about the meaning of joyfulness. Then, after his final blessing, the church soared with a powerful rendition of "O Holy Night," led by one of the parish's young sopranos.

Most of the time as I sat in my pew I thought about my mom and my dad. And also about St. Margaret of Scotland. My old man was Scot-American and my mom was Hungarian-American, and they converged within that great medieval saint known as "The Pearl of Scotland."

Whose silver religious medal was given to me by my mom at my First Communion (along with the holy card of Cardinal Mindszenty that's still in my wallet), and it's been worn around my neck ever since.

Margaret was an English princess (the granddaughter of King Edmund Ironside) who was born in Hungary in 1045. At the age of twelve, her family was called back to England since her father seemed a possible successor to the crown. But Edward died soon after arrival (maybe under suspicious circumstances?), and after the Battle of Hastings and the Norman Conquest, Margaret's mother Agatha took her children north to Northumbria. Eventually, she decided to return to the continent, but a vicious storm in 1068 shipwrecked the family further north into Scotland where they came under the protection of the Scottish King Malcolm III. Margaret was twenty-three at the time, and two years later she was married to the widower Malcolm and became Queen of Scotland.

I've read very few non-sports books in my life, but my mother made sure that I read bios of both Mindszenty and St. Margaret.

Renowned for her piety and charity, especially for orphans and the poor, Margaret apparently "civilized" her vulgar illiterate husband and ended up the mother of eight children, including three kings of Scotland (or four if you count Edmund).

So what's the deal with the Hungarian connection?

Apparently the precise lineage of Margaret's mother Agatha has been much debated by historians for the past millennia. She obviously lived in Hungary where she married Edward, and she was generally believed to be born of royal Hungarian blood. But it seems that everybody else wants to claim her as well, including the Germans (through the Holy Roman Emperors), the Russians (through the Kievan Rurikid dynasty), and even the Bulgarians and the Poles.

My mother, although readily admitting that it really didn't matter, stuck with the Hungarians. The home team. As a result, there was a portrait of St. Margaret of Scotland (and Hungary) in our home in New Brunswick and our cottage down at Sea Girt, not to mention, as already mentioned, engraved into the silver medal on a silver chain around my neck.

Near the end of "O Holy Night!" I left the church, went to my car, and watched the parishioners, flush with Christmas spirit, leave for their homes. When I felt certain that the church would be mostly empty, I went back inside and lit some candles.

For my mom.

For my father.

For Katie, and Cindy, and Angie.

And one for the one who needed help the most.

Me.

Chapter 18

St. Ladislaus

(Saturday, 12/25/21)

He came down the aisle to where I was sitting in the back pew.

"Come with me, Richard."

Maybe I shouldn't have bothered the old priest on Christmas Day, but after behaving the way I did with Cal at Sea Girt, I'd called him at the rectory and asked him if we could talk.

"When?"

"Tonight?" I tried.

He thought it over and made a suggestion.

"After Midnight Mass?"

"I'll see you then, Father."

I followed him up the main aisle, knelt as he did before the altar, then crossed the sanctuary into the sacristy. After he'd put on his winter coat and killed a few interior lights (someone had already extinguished the innumerable Christmas candles), we exited the church and went over to the rectory. Once inside, as directed, I sat on the couch in the parlor.

"Would you like a drink of something?"

"I'm good, Father."

He seemed relieved.

He removed his coat and sat down in a chair facing me, with a painting of the Sacred Heart high on the wall behind him. The holiday season and the late hour had obviously worn him down, and I felt certain that he was getting up again in a few hours for even more Christmas day Masses, yet he was still relaxed, still willing to take his time with someone he'd known since I was a child.

"I know I haven't been any help," he admitted.

He was right about that.

A few days after we'd spoken in the church after my mom's burial, he called me on the phone.

"I've been thinking over your problem, Richard, and I'd like to talk to someone who's a lot smarter than me, but I won't be able to do so until after Christmas. Is that all right with you?"

My problem, you might remember, is that I'd come to the realization that my entire life was essentially bogus.

Frivolous.

Of no account.

"That's fine, Father, it's been bothering me for a long time, and there's certainly no rush. Maybe it's something that I need to work out for myself."

"Maybe it's something that your parish priest should be able to help you with, but I don't want to throw out useless advice. Or even worse, misguided advice."

"I appreciate it, Father."

I really did.

Who wouldn't admire a man as intelligent and experienced as Fr. Nagy admitting that he didn't know the answer to every question that walked into his church.

"God bless you, Richard."

So here I was, within the dark initial hours of Christmas morning, pestering the poor old man once again, but this time I wasn't here about *that* particular problem. I had another more pressing problem.

What should I do about the Angie Anderson situation?

Was I wrong to lie and protect her privacy?

Was I wrong to let a rapist walk free?

"I've got another problem, Father."

He already knew what was going on. He'd obviously seen it on the news.

"But I thought the young woman's statement a few hours ago made it perfectly clear that it was all a misunderstanding. That there never was any assault, and that you had nothing to do with anything."

"It's not true."

He was naturally quite surprised, and he waited patiently.

"There *was* a rape, Father, but not by me, and I'm not sure what I should be doing about it."

He continued to wait for more, so I said what I probably shouldn't have said, but I said it anyway.

"Can we speak under Confessional seal?"

"Of course," he said, as if it was a given.

So I told him the whole ugly story about ten years ago. Every detail. Then I told him about Angie's visit this morning and Cal's visit this evening.

When it was over, he shook his head.

"Damn."

Which maybe a priest isn't supposed to say, but it seemed exactly appropriate at the moment.

Yes, damn.

After a bit of silence, I broke the silence and repeated myself.

"I don't know what I'm supposed to do."

He shook his head again and smiled.

"You're the worst parishioner I've ever had, Richard," he kidded, "and you're not even a parishioner anymore!"

"I know, but you're the only one I can talk to."

"I know, but you're still making me feel rather useless."

He meant it.

"I'm sorry, Father."

I meant it as well.

It was now the morning of the glorious day of the Virgin Birth, and I'm killing this old priest with intractable problems.

But he was a trouper.

"I think I know how to handle this, Richie," he decided. "I think I should pass the buck."

He laughed a bit.

"I think I should send you to the same person I was planning to talk to about your other problem. He's an old Jesuit. Very old, in fact. Probably a billion. He makes me look like a kid. He's also the smartest person on planet earth."

Which seemed like quite an exaggeration, but he said it like it was an indisputable fact.

"I'll text you his address tomorrow. He's up in Paterson, and you should go visit him Thursday night at ten o'clock. I meet with him once a month for advice and Confession, and I'll let him know that you're coming, and you can talk to him about both of your dilemmas."

It sounded like a plan, even if it sounded like an odd one.

"Fine, I'll be there at ten o'clock."

Good, now I need to get some sleep. There's nothing more comforting than passing the buck."

I smiled, we stood up, and we walked to the rectory door.

When I stepped out into the cold Christmas night, I turned around, and we shook hands.

"Your worst non-parishioner says thanks, Father."

He laughed.

"Oh, and one more thing, Richard."

I waited for his one more thing.

"Don't be offended."

Which seemed rather curious,

"What do you mean?"

He shrugged.

"He doesn't suffer fools."

Which didn't come out exactly right, but I wasn't offended.

"Is that what I am?" I kidded.

"That's what we *all* are," he said.

Dead serious.

Then the rectory door shut, and I was right back where I started.

Oh, well.

Feliz Navidad!

Chapter 19

Stone Tower

(Thursday, 12/30/21)

The old guy lives at the top of a stone tower.

No kidding.

Way up on Garret Mountain, high above Paterson, New Jersey.

I'm not making this up.

On the day after Christmas, Father Nagy texted me his address, if that's what you'd call it.

> *Fr. John C. Colt: Take the long drive off Valley Road up Garret Mountain past Lambert Castle. Above the castle, there's a related stone tower. Enter at the only entrance and go up the stone stairs to the cell at the top. Good luck!*

"Cell"?

"Good luck"?

"Colt"?

Was it too much of a reach to suspect that the old priest was related to Jack Colt, the famous NJ private detective who'd solved, among other sensational cases, "The Little Girl Killer Case" and the "Haunted House Murders"? And whose rude receptionist once recommended Mack Dawson to me eleven years ago?

Curious, I Googled the old priest and printed out his Wiki page.

Twenty-six pages long!

Sure enough, he was some kind of great-great uncle of Jack Colt, who'd apparently been named in his honor. Apparently the two of them are the last remaining of the New Jersey Colts, who descended from the famous Samuel Colt family of gunsmiths.

Monsignor Colt was a very well-connected Jesuit, who preferred the term "Ignatian." A brilliant theologian and traditionalist moral philosopher, he'd worked in the Vatican for many years under Cardinal Ratzinger, who later became Pope Benedict XVI. Eventually, Monsignor Colt came back to his native Paterson in 2014 "to die in peace," but he obviously hadn't died yet. He lives as a hermit in Lambert Tower, visited by various friends and religious.

Including, apparently, Fr. Nagy.

I parked near the castle (yes, Paterson, New Jersey, has a castle) and made my way through the chilling darkness up to the stone tower and entered through its metal door. It was pitch black inside so I used my cell phone light as I climbed the steep stone steps. At the top, I knocked on the wooden door and announced myself.

Somewhat warily.

"It's Richard Ramsey."

"Well, I'm certainly glad it's not some serial killer."

It was unclear if it was intended as humor or condescension.

Maybe both.

Somehow, illogically, within his wiseassed comment, I could also sense an eerie erudition.

Or maybe it was just my imagination.

I opened the door and stepped inside the tiny cell.

It was pitch black.

In the light of my cell phone's light, there was a tiny wizened man dressed in priestly blacks and a white collar sitting on a tiny cot with his back against the stone wall.

No pillows.

Not much of anything.

No sink, no bathroom, no refrigerator, no air conditioner, no heating vents, just a small wooden table, two wooden chairs, and a few books.

"Are you smart enough to have figured out that I'm blind as a bat?"

I hadn't.

I guess the books were braille.

"Of course," I lied.

"Lie number one," he said without hesitation. "Now come over here so I can feel your head and see how smart you are."

What?

I did as I was told.

I slipped off my eye patch then leaned over his cot and announced my head's presence.

"Here."

He reached up his small bony hands, ran his fingers over my face, then pressed his fingertips across the top of my head.

"Good," he said, "above average."

"Well, that's refreshing to know," I said. "I thought phrenology had been debunked over a century ago."

Like him, I'd also grown up a New Jersey wiseass.

He smiled a barely discernable smile.

"When did you lose your left eye?" he asked.

It was obviously a case of the blind questioning the partially blind. I guess he must have felt the little ridges in my forehead left by my eye patch's strap.

"A line drive in my junior year. I was playing third base."

I waited for some kind of inappropriate response.

"Was he out?"

Oddly enough, he was. After smashing into my face, the ball dropped down into my glove.

Entirely by accident.

"Yes."

He nodded an indecipherable nod.

"All right, Richard, sit down in a chair so you can start whining about your horribly difficult life. Tell me about all the terrible and insurmountable obstacles that you've faced as a healthy semi-educated one-eyed American living in the most pampered living conditions in the history of the world."

What had Fr. Nagy warned me?

Don't be offended by him.

Fine. I won't be.

I sat down in one of his chairs.

"You can light a candle if you don't want to burn off the battery of your stupid cell phone."

How he knew the little light was on I have no idea. I thought he was "blind as a bat."

"Fine," I said as I lit a small candle on the little wooden table.

"When Fr. Nagy told me that you have some unsolvable problems, I asked him why he was sending you to me since your problems are unsolvable. Guess what he said? He said, 'How else am I supposed to get rid of him?'"

My "take no offence" vow didn't last very long.

"Lie number one," I said. "He's a good man, and he'd *never* say anything like that, you old corpse."

I regretted it as soon as I'd said it, but the old boy smiled again in the faint candlelight.

"Well, *that's* coming soon enough," he said, in reference to my corpse reference, "and you're right that he didn't say it exactly like that. I extrapolated a bit. Artistic freedom. What he really said was, 'Well, I still hope you can give him some direction.'"

"That's quite an extrapolation," I pointed out.

"Well, it's at least comforting to learn that you know the meaning of the word."

"Can you help me?" I asked, referring to my problems.

"I'll have to hear them first."

I was quite surprised that Fr. Nagy hadn't prepared him. Maybe he thought that it would be best if I tried to explain my problems myself, which I had my doubts about, but I was willing to try.

Besides, I was kind of enjoying the old Ignatian's rudeness. It was refreshing in a New Jersey kind of way.

"It'll take a while," I warned him.

"Should I call the Bonfire Lounge down in Paterson and cancel my salsa date?"

I laughed.

"Maybe you should."

So I started with Angie's rape.

As with Fr. Nagy in the rectory on Christmas morning, I told him everything in great detail. He listened patiently, and he never interrupted to ask a question. Maybe he was asleep. Maybe he was dead. Either which way, his eyes were definitely dead, and his tiny wizened body was motionless.

I finished.

He said nothing, so I did.

"Obviously, I don't know what to do."

I'd done my best, and I was eager to hear whatever "the smartest person on planet earth" might have to say.

"Have you prayed?" he asked.

It threw me a bit, but I responded anyway.

"Yes."

"A lot?"

"Maybe not as much as I should have."

"Try more."

Was that it?

Had I driven all the way up here to Insult Tower from Sea Girt to be told to pray.

I tried not to show my irritation.

"What's your other problem?" he asked.

I was stunned.

"Are we really moving on to my 'other' problem?"

"I'll be the judge of that, sonny. How am I supposed to know if they're related or not?"

Which seemed both reasonable and unreasonable at the same time.

So I told him my "life" problem, which was a hell of a lot harder to do given that the man seemed to lack any kind of human sympathy for human weaknesses, but I did my best.

Let's face it, how do you tell a man as accomplished as the half-dead Ignatian lying in front of me that you're unhappy with your life? That you feel as though both your life and your work is frivolous. That you worry that you've been wasting God's precious time?

It certainly wasn't easy, but I said to myself, the hell with it, I'm going to tell the old bastard exactly how I feel.

Which I did, just as I'd done with Fr. Nagy, and the old Ignatian listened patiently without a single interruption.

When I finished, there was nothing but silence as we stared at each other across the small wooden table from our own dark peripheries of the tiny candle's flame.

"That's rather serious, young man."

I was quite relieved that he took me seriously.

"What will God say," I asked, "about a man who does nothing but watch games and then makes meaningless comments about them?"

"I doubt that He'll be pleased."

Great, now we were getting somewhere.

"This is what I'd like you to do," he began, as I sat in the darkness of the stone tower waiting, as they say, with bated breath. "Read *Willie Mays Summer: 1954*, then go see Dr. Rankin."

What!

More sports?

More passing the buck?

The old goat wants me to go visit Robert Rankin, whom I knew from nowhere, although I'd naturally heard about his book about the Giants' championship season in 1954. It had come out a few years ago, and I'd been intending to read it, but I'd never gotten around to it. Now, it seemed, I'd definitely be reading it.

I guess.

"Is that the best you've got, old man?"

He smiled yet another smile which I was unable to discern the meaning of.

"You'd like more, young Richard? Fine. Read the *Philothea*, specifically Section One, Chapters Three and Twenty-Three, and Section Three, Chapter Thirty-One."

I didn't know whether to get angry or laugh.

Was this some kind of Joke?

"What the hell is the *Philothea*?" I mispronounced.

He shrugged.

"You'll figure it out. I checked out your head earlier."

Meaning my brain capacity.

I guess I was getting angry.

"I'd like a lot more than three chapters of a book I've never heard of and a book about Willie Mays."

He seemed unconcerned.

Entirely unconcerned.

"Fine. You want more homework? Fine. I want you to write about your life and your recent problems, and I want you to write it like a novel, and then bring it back to me. And since I'm a big sports fan myself, include some of those quotes that Fr. Nagy told me that you've been collecting. Actually, let's be even more specific than that. Include at least seven classics quotes along with your seven personal favorites for each of my favorite sports, as well as your top-three All-Time Greatest lists for hardball, football, roundball, and the sweet science. And throw in some nicknames too. And make the whole bloody thing somewhere between two-hundred-and-fifty and three-hundred-and-fifty pages, with no skimping, then bring it back to me before Easter."

Was the guy messing with me?

"Are you busting my balls?"

"I'm trying to help you."

Oddly enough, I could tell that he meant it.

"But I know nothing about novels, I'm a sportswriter."

"Well, surely, you've read *The Sportswriter*?"

"I started it once."

Naturally, I'd once tried reading the novel with a title like that. It was published back in 1986 by Richard Ford, and it was about a sportswriter who was divorced, had "issues," and lived in New Jersey. (Sound like somebody you know?) Despite its misleading title, there was very little about sports in the book, so I bailed about sixty pages in. The guy could obviously write, but I wasn't interested in the problems of the main character Frank Bascombe, a mediocrity who actually joined a "Divorced Men's Club," and who was apparently featured in three more of Ford's novels, one of which won the Pulitzer (*Independence Day*), and who (Bascombe) ended up a realtor in (I think) Florida.

The truth is I know nothing about novels.

Repeat: nothing!

When I told my film crit pal Simon about my attempt to read *The Sportswriter*, he shook his head sadly and said:

"You know *that* happened to me one time, Richie. Some guy named Walker Percy had written a novel called *The Moviegoer*, and I was anxious to read it, but it had almost nothing about movies in it."

The priest jarred me out of my befuddlement.

"By Easter," he reaffirmed.

I shook my head in acquiescence.

What else was I supposed to do?

I needed help.

"You know," he said, "I love good sports quotes."

Great.

I came to this stone coffin for moral guidance, and I'd run into another sports nut.

Even though I was entirely unresponsive, it didn't slow him down a bit.

"You want the hear my favorite, Richard?"

"Sure."

Why not?

"It's from Mike Ditka."

In case you don't know, Mike Ditka was a tough-guy Hall of Fame tight end and later the tough-guy coach of the tough-guy Chicago Bears.

He recited the quote like scripture:

What's the difference between a three-week-old puppy and a sportswriter? In six weeks, the puppy stops whining.

Well, I guess it's not a huge leap to assume that the Ditka quote was directed directly at me, but at this point I didn't care in the least.

I'd been given my "assignments," and I wanted to get the hell out of there.

He wanted me out too.

"Kneel down for your blessing, young man," he said, "then squelch the candle flame on the way out and be careful on the stone stairs."

I did as I was told.

I was happy to be outside in the freezing cold.

Chapter 20

New Year's Eve

(Friday, 12/31/21)

Film, film, and more film.

What else did I expect?

Simon had convinced me, now that the press was no longer hounding me about the Angie Anderson case, to come to his annual New Year's Eve party at his loft on Broome Street in SoHo.

I agreed.

But I had my own motivations.

Earlier, I'd spent the day at home in New Brunswick watching the bowl games.

Gator Bowl (11:00), Wake Forest beats Rutgers
(damn!)
Cotton Bowl (3:30), Alabama beats Cincinnati
(roll Tide!)
Orange Bowl (7:30), Georgia beats Michigan

(fine with me)

Somewhere during the halftime of the 'Bama game, it dawned on me that I might actually be "addicted" to sports. Why not? Even today, with all the serious stuff that was going on in my life, I still couldn't resist spending the entire day watching young men play football games. I know it might seem silly at first, but people get addicted to all kinds of things. Booze, drugs, nicotine, gambling, porn, shopping, sex, video games, etc. We live in a nation where almost every single person is clearly addicted to their cell phones. Let's face it, every time one of those little phones rings, no matter where its owner might be at the moment, he/she jerks to attention like a pigeon in a Skinner Box, feeling utterly compelled to check yet another (almost invariably) meaningless text.

So I went into my parents' rather extensive library and snooped around. Fr. Hardon's excellent *Modern Catholic Dictionary* defines addiction as:

> *The state of being physically dependent on something, generally alcohol or drugs, but it can be any material object or experience.*

The word, as noted, derives from the Latin *addicere*, meaning "to give one's consent to a thing."

Far be it from me to attempt to emend the great moral theologian, but I might add being "psychologically" dependent as well, although the more I thought about being "physically dependent," I realized that it would have definitely affected me physiologically if I'd been somehow prevented from watching the three bowl games today. After all, despite my scattershot research in the family library, I was still craving the second half of the Alabama game, and I would have felt not only psychologically deprived but also physically lousy if I'd been deprived of the opportunity to watch the rest of the game.

Which is called, as everyone knows, withdrawal.

A well-known symptom of addiction.

Sure addiction's more easily witnessed with drugs and alcohol, but did you ever watch a compulsive gambler who was unable to place his bets? Or a teenage kid who's deprived of his video games?

These surely simplistic speculations were in no way intended to compare my situation with someone lost in the horrors of alcohol dependency, and it was definitely not some self-serving scheme to justify my bad behavior by using the word "addiction" to convince myself that I had no control over my actions.

It was simply a thought.

A possibility.

Maybe a realization.

Addiction leads to harmful behaviors, and, in the Christian sense, it damages our relationship with God and our relationships with others. Such as my marriage with Cindy. Such as my relationship with my now deceased girlfriend Katie. As with others as well. All of whom, for some idiotic reason (some personal failing on my part, some willful sinfulness) always ranked second in my life after my sports obsession.

As one Catholic commentator on the web had pointed out, addiction limits our freedom and creates a distorted outlook on the world which encourages a disregard for others.

The symptoms are well-known, and I took special notice of the ones that were most relevant to my own situation.

Intense cravings for the habit
Isolation from others
Neglecting responsibilities
Withdrawal when deprived
Etc.

All the recommendations were familiar as well: admission, prayer, temperance, counseling, etc.

Well, I've already been seeking counseling, even climbing the stone steps of a stone tower to be told by a half-dead priest to read a book about baseball!

The timer on my cell went off. Halftime was almost over. I shut the books, left the library, and went back to the Alabama game.

Roll Tide!

Then onto the Orange Bowl!

As soon as the game was over, I had a taxi waiting to drive me into Manhattan, where I took the subway down to SoHo. Arriving late at one of Simon's parties was no big deal. It was to be expected. I'd been to many of Simon's New Year's Eve bashes before, and even though I really didn't feel like it tonight, they were always enjoyable affairs, flush with New York film people and a nice way to "champagne in" the coming year.

Simon Gerard was an old friend. But ironically we *didn't* meet at a sports venue (his only on-and-off sports interest was Australian rugby), and we *didn't* meet at a film screening (given my general disinterest). We met about ten years ago at Malone's Irish Bar on Third Avenue, where we met literally at the bar. I'd been over at Citi Field for a Mets' day game, and I'd stopped off to have a drink at Malone's, when I ran into a very chatty Aussie. We were both ordering whiskey sours, which led to a discussion about the pleasures of whiskey sours, which led to the even more active pleasure of drinking more and more delicious sours.

Which led to our friendship.

Simon was new in the city at the time. From Tasmania. Yes, Tasmania. He'd done some film reviewing for *FilmInk* back home, and now he had a new position at *New York Magazine*. He was an expert on the Australian New Wave of the 1970s and early 1980s (before both of us were born), and he was already the respected author of *Bruce Beresford: Auteur* and *The Australian Film Renaissance*.

We were very different, of course. Simon, a very contented bachelor, was exuberant, charming, witty, and gregarious. I was (well, you know what I am) much more pensive, more self-composed, more private. He also had no interest in my only interest, and I had no interest in his only interest. Nevertheless, he insisted that I watch at least five New Wave films "so we could possibly be friends," to which I agreed if he would go with me to see a Mets game and a Jets game "so we could possibly be friends." I suspect that I enjoyed the films more than he did the Mets and the Jets, but he was always a good sport about it, and we had fun as always.

Since that first night at Malone's, we've remained in touch as our careers moved forward accordingly. Eventually, Simon started reviewing for *NR* as well as writing occasional pieces for *The Hollywood Reporter*, even though he only went to California once a year, on a three day stop-over on his way back home to visit his family in Tasmania. He'd become a bit of a film iconoclast, a controversial maverick, and his last two books, *The Death of Serious Cinema* and *Why Television is Better than Film*, were hugely influential, much debated, and much attacked (which he much enjoyed).

Tonight, as always, his impressive loft was packed. I won't bother to drop names, but let's just say that there were more than a few bigshot film directors and actors knocking off Simon's Dom Perignon. I avoided them as best I could, knocked off a few glasses of Perignon myself, and did my best to be congenial, circulate, and mingle. Much of the time accompanied by Simon's current girlfriend, Jasmine, whom I'm sure he'd asked to make sure that I was comfortable despite being out of my element.

Film, film, and more film.

Occasionally, politics would rear its ugly head somewhere in the room, and I'd run for the hills. Otherwise, it was all about film. There was an odd yet quite pleasant vacuum of any kind of sports talk.

None, in fact.

It was like being on another planet.

Where I was the alien.

They were constantly referencing all kinds of films, both new and old, that I'd never heard of, so I just nodded politely and drank more champagne. Eventually, I made my way over to Simon who was entertaining a small group of admirers with his infectious banter. When he saw me, he stopped everything and gave me a big hug.

"Just what I need," I kidded, "a phony Hollywood hug."

He laughed.

"No, Ritchie, that was a serious SoHo hug. I'll explain the difference later. I'm so glad you came!"

He meant it. He knew about my mom, and he knew about Katie, and we'd already talked things over on the phone. I think he was worried that I was brooding about things, and he wanted to get me out of the house.

Quickly I was introduced to his small group of sycophants, none of whom seem to recognize me as the sportswriter in the recent news who'd been the suspect in a rape case.

For which I was grateful.

All of which seemed especially odd given that my black eye patch is pretty hard to miss, and my photo had been plastered all over the web as well as the print papers.

After introductions, the other guests immediately got back to where they were before my interruption.

Film.

A pretty young woman in a slinky black dress asked Simon:

"But it wasn't *really* a 'renaissance' was it, Simon?" she said, which seemed to me a surprisingly good question.

"No, love," he agreed, "not if the word means rebirth, but I liked the sound of it. But you're right, Aussie cinema was dead and dormant until *Walkabout* in 1971."

That's one that I'd seen. Lots of dry brown Australian outback and lots and lots of walking. Oddly enough I'd stumbled into a film conversation that I could actually follow a bit, even though I had no intention of participating.

"How did it happen?" an elderly professorial type (NYU? New School? CUNY?) with a long and ugly grey-streaked ponytail asked.

Hell, even *I* knew the answer to that one!

"Money, Trevor, isn't it always money? After the big war, the Gorton government started funding the moribund industry, most significantly by training young director wannabes, which eventually paid off in the Seventies."

The little black dress was back.

"Which ones should I watch?"

I was quite impressed by her admission that she didn't know something about film in a loft full of film aficionados and more than a few film snobs.

Simon looked over at me.

"Maybe I should let Professor Ramsey give his opinion."

Now *I* was a professor.

I played along.

"All right, you bastard," I agreed.

Then I listed the same five films that Simon had required me to screen many years ago. I was surprised that I could actually still remember the names.

Walkabout
Breaker Morant
Gallipoli
Mad Max 2 (aka *The Road Warrior*)

The Year of Living Dangerously

"Which is the best?" the real professor wondered.

Once again, Simon looked at me.

Given that Simon was the world expert on Bruce Beresford who'd established himself with (and got an Oscar nom for) *Breaker Morant,* it might have been a bit awkward for me to mention any of the other four films.

But no problem.

I could be totally honest.

"*Breaker,*" I decided, a bit full of myself.

As well as full of champagne.

"Why?" the pretty woman asked, ruining all the fun.

So I stumbled my way through some gibberish.

"Tour de force acting, especially by Edward Woodward, brilliant photography, and powerful subject matter about a possible war crime during the Boer War."

I was especially pleased with my pretentious usage of the term "tour de force." I couldn't help noticing that Simon was smiling.

Then the New School guy looked at Simon.

"That was Beresford, right?"

"It was," Simon said, keeping it modest and simple. For years, he'd been making the case that Beresford was the greatest film director alive. Simon's father had known Beresford when they were undergrads at the University of Sydney, along with Clive James, Germaine Greer, and Les Murray. All of whom also went on to be famous in one capacity or another. As for Simon, he'd be the first to admit that Beresford had made his share of stinkers, which the director has admitted himself, but his best films, according to Simon, put him in a class by himself.

Breaker Morant
Tender Mercies (Best Director, Best Actor for Robert Duval)
Driving Miss Daisy (Best Picture)
Double Jeopardy (which Katie loved)
Evelyn (which Cindy loves)

It always sounded pretty convincing to me, but I'm essentially a film idiot.

As his group was pondering their next interrogation, I made my move. It was getting close to midnight, and I wanted to get to my real reason for coming to the party tonight.

I looked over at Simon.

"Can we talk?"

"Of course!"

He smoothly disengaged from his little audience with all the grace and good spirits of a politician leading by ten points in the polls.

"Come along with me," he said.

He obviously sensed that I wanted some privacy, so he led me over to a pair of huge French windows, opened the one on the right, and we stepped out onto a small balcony overhanging Broome Street. The night was cold but comforting, and the new year was only twenty minutes away.

"What's up, mate?"

"I want to ask you about film."

He laughed.

"Yeah, that'll be the day. Why not tell me how you're doing after all this Hoboken ruckus."

"I'm fine, Simon," I lied, "but it might not be over."

"Should I ask?"

"I can't get into it right now, but I can assure you that I did nothing wrong."

"I've never had any doubt about that. So what's on your mind? I'll need to get back in there before the damned ball comes down."

"I want to ask you about film," I repeated.

Now he was curious, so he waited for me to take it wherever it was going.

"Would it be fair to say," I asked, "that you're obsessed with film?"

He laughed.

"I'm not sure if obsessed is a strong enough word, Richie."

"But doesn't it narrow down your life?"

It was a serious question, and he took it seriously.

"Yes, I suppose it does."

"Do you ever wonder if it's too much? If it's too inhibiting? If it's too confining?"

He shrugged.

"Not really, Richie. I suppose it does do all of those things, but who cares, right?"

I pressed ahead.

"Do you feel that you're happy with the life you have?"

"Yes, I guess I am, Richie, now that you've forced me to think about it. I really can't imagine doing anything else. Or even wanting to do anything else. I guess I'm, as you Christians like to say, blessed."

Simon was a quiet agnostic.

Actually, he was an admitted heathen.

He took a drink of Perignon.

"I guess, Richie," he continued, "that we're really talking about you, right?"

"Yes. I feel that I lead a rather frivolous life. A life of little or no consequence."

He shrugged again.

"But isn't that," he decided, "if we really think about it, the human condition?"

"Does it have to be?"

He put his hand on my shoulder, and he looked into my eyes.

Friend to friend.

"Look, pal, you need to see a priest."

"I've already seen two."

He laughed, and so did I.

In the comfortable silence on the balcony, we could hear the music from the party inside the French windows.

Beyonce, I think.

He nodded at his loft.

"It's time for me to get back in there and get frivolous."

"Sounds good to me. Let's do it."

We were soon back inside the packed loft as Simon shut off the lights and led a loud countdown to 2022 in conjunction with the dropping of the Times Square ball, which everyone was watching on Simon's huge OLED television screen. Everyone was loud, animated, raucous, and a bit more than tipsy.

And seemingly happy.

I stood within the crowd as anonymously as possible.

Three, two, one!

Everyone cheered, couples kissed, and others quaffed more champagne.

Within the darkness, someone came close and kissed me warmly on the mouth. Then she was gone. Except for her perfume. Maybe it was the pretty woman in the little black dress.

Maybe not.

In a way, it summed up my life.

It was time to get my drunken ass back to New Jersey.

II.

2022

Chapter 21

New Year's Day

(Saturday, 1/1/22)

I gave the guy a New Year's Eve tip.

I was still feeling pretty looped from Simon's New Year's bash, still tasting that anonymous midnight kiss, which was pretty ridiculous. Which, I guess, indicates how much Perignon I'd had.

I was feeling good. I guess booze can do that. It couldn't eliminate my problems, but it had certainly mitigated them. Even the fact that my secret mission had failed didn't seem to bother me. So what if Simon was perfectly happy with his obsession? What else did I expect?

The old guy driving the cab was obviously pleased.

"Thank you, sir," he said with sincerity, with an unrecognizable accent, "have a Happy New Year!"

"You too," I reciprocated, "you too!"

I got out of the cab into the dark new night of 2022. Who knows, maybe it would be a better year. I stood in the cold in front of my New

Brunswick home and watched the cab drive down Lorain Street and vanish into the darkness.

Then I hear a sound from behind me. A kind of rushing sound.

Then I was struck on the back of the head. I'm sure the booze helped, but it still hurt like hell. I bent over as various other sucker punches struck the side of my face, as I tried to cover up. I was helpless and disoriented. Soon I was down on the pavement being relentlessly kicked. Mostly into my sides.

It was all a furious blur, but I do remember hearing the word "asshole," which was obviously directed at me. It seemed that I'd been blindsided by two assailants, and I could definitely smell the booze.

Whiskey.

"Get his wallet," I heard one say to the other as the kicking continued. Then I felt his hands searching for my wallet at the back pocket of my jeans. Instinctively, I tried to resist and struggled with the assailant. Even though it was pitch black out, I could see his black ski mask. Then I felt another powerful blow right into my face, and I believe that I blacked out. A few minutes later, I woke up in the gutter, dripping warm blood from my face.

I looked up Lorain Street and saw the black SUV driving away into the night

Then I blacked out again.

Chapter 22

Cove Point

(Friday, 1/21/22)

I looked out at the dark Chesapeake with an uneasy foreboding, then I knocked on the cottage door.

It was nearly three weeks since I'd woken up in a hospital bed in St. Peter's with a pretty young cop staring down at me.

"Can you talk?"

I shrugged.

Then I felt the pain, and I winced or groaned or both.

"Should I call a nurse?" she asked with concern.

"That might be a good idea," I understated.

After all, there's nothing like a hit of morphine for a pleasant trip into painless oblivion.

Eventually, I did give the young cop an account of what had happened when I was attacked, but it was essentially worthless. All I really knew was that there were two of them, that they attempted to get my wallet, and that they drove away in a non-descript SUV.

It seemed that I was the world's most useless victim.

As for my injuries, there were multiple lacerations on my face (twenty stitches that seem to be healing up nicely), two cracked ribs (*very* painful, please avoid at all costs), a ruptured kidney (which managed to recoup itself after five days of bloody urine), and a whole bunch of minor yet scarily grotesque contusions.

I stayed in St. Peter's for three days, and I was a model patient. As unpleasant as the whole thing was, it distracted me from all the other crap in my life, so it seemed like an odd kind of blessing. As my mother had once taught me, I offered up my various and lingering pains for the blackened souls of my assailants, in the hope that they would eventually amend their ways and find the same bloody light that I was searching for.

The attackers, of course, were never found, but at least I'd managed to keep my wallet.

The most minor of minor victories!

I recouped at home, read Rankin's *Willie Mays Summer: 1954*, and enjoyed the hell out of it. I had no idea what the half-dead priest in the tower was up to (or how further indulging in sports would somehow help me with my sports obsession), but my first assignment was certainly a pleasurable one. The author, Robert Rankin, had written the book for his father who'd died of pancreatic cancer in 2016. His old man had grown up a Willie Mays fanatic because *his* old man (the grandfather) had also been a Willie fanatic who was actually at the Polo Grounds when Willie made his famous Vic Wertz catch in the first game of the 1954 World Series.

It was a beautiful book, a beautiful tribute to the New York Giants, to 1950s baseball in New York City, to the guys on the team, and to Willie Mays. It was full of marvelous stories, many of which I'd never heard before even though I knew an awful lot about Willie Mays. Unlike the edginess of my own books, Rankin's *Willie Mays Summer* was warm and charming and irresistible. Somewhat in the mode of Roger Kahn's famous memoir *The Boys of Summer* about the Brooklyn Dodgers in 1955.

So maybe *that* was the old priest's message?

Mellow out?

Be more like Rankin?

Be more like Kahn?

I doubted it, but who knows.

Then I googled Rankin.

He was hardly what I expected.

The guy was a canon lawyer!

He was also a professor in the Theology Department at Georgetown University who'd written books like *Trent: The Twenty-fifth Session* and *The Canonization of St. Ulrich*.

Who the hell was St. Ulrich?

Rankin was also a Jersey guy like me (growing up in Wayne, New Jersey) who also went to Rutgers! After that, and after some kind of personal life reevaluation, he studied at the Pontifical Gregorian University in Rome before completing his PhD in Canon Law at Catholic University. Two years ago, he'd been appointed by Archbishop Mackenzie of the Washington Diocese to serve as Vice-Postulator (devil's advocate) in the canonization cause of Venerable Adelaide

Bruckner, a pious Maryland "miracle worker" nun (1945-1972). The various accounts on the web were somewhat vague about the current status of the case. Regardless, Robert ("everyone calls me Robbie") Rankin, was not only well-connected ecclesiastically, but theologically grounded.

Maybe that was why the old Jesuit had sent me to Maryland to meet with Rankin?

For some non-prelate moral direction?

Because Rankin had once turned his own life around?

Because he was a Jersey guy?

Maybe.

I really didn't know, and to be honest, I really didn't care. I just wanted to meet the guy who'd written *Willie Mays Summer* for his father, just as I'd written *Amazin'* for my old man.

When I got a hold of Rankin's office number at Georgetown, I called him, and he picked up.

"Robbie Rankin."

I did my best to explain the unexplainable.

"My name is Richard Ramsey, and I've been told to talk to you by an old Jesuit."

There was silence on the line.

I think I could actually hear him thinking.

"The Richard Ramsey who wrote *Amazin'*?"

"Yes."

"Loved that book!" he said with enthusiasm. "As I'm sure everyone tells you, that book was amazing!"

I laughed.

"Yeah, I think I've heard that one before."

"I'll be glad to meet with you Richard, even though I have no idea what we're meeting about."

"Me neither."

Now it was his turn to laugh.

"Who's behind all this?"

"Some old Ignatian named Colt, like the gunsmiths."

He seemed astonished and incredibly impressed.

"Did you actually meet him?"

"Yes."

"Up in his tower?"

"Yes, you've heard of him?"

"Of course, the man's a legend. He's also a saint."

"Well, the old bastard that I met certainly didn't seem like a saint."

He laughed again.

"Yeah, I've heard he's got a few rough edges."

"He's *nothing* but edges. All sharp ones."

He thought it over.

"Why don't you come out to my house? I live in Cove Point in Maryland. It'll be much more comfortable than my office."

"Sounds good to me."

So we set the time (today), and I flew down to Dulles, rented a Ford Bronco, and drove out to Cove Point in Calvert County where I'd never been before.

The little cottage where Robbie lived with his wife Ronnie and their young child faces the Chesapeake north of the Cove Point Lighthouse. It was now evening, and the world was covered with a light dusting of snow that glowed in the dazzling moonlight. It seemed odd to be showing up at the home of someone I didn't even know with a bottle of Gevrey-Chambertin Pinot Noir (recommended by the old guy working in the airport liquor store since I know nothing about wines), but Robbie insisted that his wife Ronnie had insisted that I should come for dinner at seven, and I didn't want to say no.

I texted him back:

Sounds great.

There was a follow up text.

Pot roast ok?

My mom used to make a badass yummy pot roast.

Perfect.

He opened the door.

Rankin was a few inches taller than me and handsomer than me, with dark hair and brown eyes. Tall, trim, and welcoming.

"Welcome, Richard."

I handed him the bottle.

"Do you drink this stuff?" I wondered.

"Sure, later tonight."

He held the door open, and I stepped inside. The place was small, but it reminded me of my parents' place. It was cozy, comfortable, warm, and unpretentious.

Ronnie came out of the kitchen.

She was pregnant.

I don't know why I was surprised, but I was.

She was also a very pretty blonde with very blue eyes and a lovely smile.

"Welcome to our little home," she said.

We shook hands.

She was wearing a white apron over an attractive green housedress with a white collar. Then she turned around and called for her two-year old.

"Kit? Where are you?"

The kid soon waddled into the living room with a big smile. Sportswriters never get to use the word "adorable," so here goes. This little Rankin kid, in his red flannels, was adorable.

Naturally curious, the kid pointed at my eye patch.

"Hurt?" he asked.

I knelt down in front of him.

"No, Kit, I'm fine," I assured him.

He reached out, put his hands to the sides of my face, and kissed my cheek."

I was amazed.

Taken aback.

Since I know absolutely nothing about kids.

"Thank you," I said rather stupidly.

"He's our little miracle," Ronnie explained, as I stood up again, "but I've got something going in the oven!"

Then she took her child's small hand and vanished back into the kitchen, as I sat down on the living room couch.

"Would you like a drink of something?" Robbie asked.

"Sure, what do *you* like?"

"I'm big on CC and ginger."

"Sounds good to me."

When Robbie left me alone to get the drinks, I looked around the room. There was a picture of St. Margaret on the wall, which I suppose wasn't that much of a coincidence (or was it?) given the fact that he was a "Rankin" and certainly had deep Scot roots. There were also lots of books on the bookshelves, but only one sitting on top of the coffee table.

An Introduction to the Devout Life by St. Francis de Sales.

Who was the patron saint of writers and journalists, whom my father had cited on my "Statement of Intention" back when I was fifteen years old and planning to be a sportswriter.

Do not look forward in fear to the changes in life.

Which was not the end of the coincidences.

The saint's book is also known as the *Philothea* ("Lover of God"), which the old Jesuit had told me to read from.

Which I hadn't done yet.

Naturally, I was confused.

Robbie returned with our drinks and handed me mine.

"Cheers!" he said, as he sat down in a nearby chair, and I tried his Canadian Club drowned with ginger ale.

It was delicious.

It was also time to talk.

"Have you ever met Fr. Colt?" I asked.

"Never. I wish I could, but I understand that he's on death's door."

"Apparently he's been on death's door for decades."

He laughed.

"So I've heard."

"Have you ever communicated with him?"

I hoped that it didn't sound like an interrogation, but Robbie seemed fine with my questions.

"Never, and I have no idea why he sent you to me."

I pointed down at the *Philothea*.

"Are you reading St. Francis?"

"Yes, Ronnie and I are reading it together. A few pages every night. Have you ever read it?"

"No, but Fr. Colt told me to read a few sections of the book, which I definitely intend to read as soon as I get back to New Jersey."

Robbie didn't seem to think it was odd at all.

"The book was recommended to me by Bishop Mackenzie, who's a protégé of Fr. Colt. So I guess it's not an unlikely book for priests like them to recommend to people who might need it."

"I guess not."

Robbie looked at me, and I looked at him.

"Do you have any idea what we're supposed to do?" he asked.

"Not a clue," I assured him.

So we did what most men who don't know each other do, we talked about sports.

He talked about how much he liked my book, and I talked about how much I liked his book.

"Willie was the best," I said, summing up everything.

"Yeah, the Say-Hey Kid. I wish I could have seen him play."

We both nodded profoundly.

"By the way," he continued, "I've ordered *Nicks*. After all, who doesn't love sports nicknames?"

"You got some favorites?"

"Sure, the Babe, the Big Train, Smokin' Joe, the Golden Jet . . . ."

Then he asked me for a few.

[Which was my opening. So here, as required, are the seven classic nicks along with my seven favorites.]

Baseball Classics:

Shoeless Joe Jackson

The Big Train (Walter Johnson)

Babe Ruth

The Iron Horse (Lou Gehrig)

Stan the Man Musial

The Say Hey Kid (Willie Mays)

Hammerin' Hank Aaron

Personal favorites:

Cool Papa Bell

Dr. Strangeglove (Dick Stuart)

The Ryan Express (Nolan Ryan)

The Barber (Sal Maglie)

King Kong Keller

Bill Spaceman Lee

Dennis Oil Can Boyd

Boxing Classics:

Gentleman Jim Corbett

The Brown Bomber (Joe Louis)

Sugar Ray Robinson

The Bronx Bull (Jake LaMotta)

Jersey Joe Walcott

Smokin' Joe Frazier

The Hit Man (Tommy Hearns)

Personal favorites:

The Wild Bull of the Pampas (Luis Firpo)

Homicide Hank (Henry Armstrong)

The Old Mongoose (Archie Moore)

The Executioner (Bernard Hopkins)

The Baby-face Assassin (Marco Antonio Barrera)

The Bodysnatcher (Mike McCallum)

Butterbean (Eric Esch)

[This all seems (dare I use the word) rather frivolous, old man. Why don't you just order my damned book and read it for yourself. It's called *Nicks: Sports Nicknames*, available at Amazon, etc.)

Football Classics:

Night Train Lane
The Galloping Ghost (Red Grange)
First Down Jimmy Brown
Broadway Joe Namath
Roger the Dodger Staubach
Jim Machine Gun Kelly
Mean Joe Green

Personal favorites:

Crazy Legs Hirsch
Bullet Bob Hayes
The Manster (Reggie White)
William the Refrigerator Perry
Megatron (Calvin Johnson)
Beast Mode (Marshawn Lynch)
The Nigerian Nightmare (Christian Okoye)

[Oops, I guess it slipped my mind, old man, that you're (as you've described yourself) "blind as a bat." So maybe you could get someone to read the book to you out loud. Hell, I'll drive up there again some-

time and read it to you. Why waste time talking about my moral failings
when we can toss around dumb nicknames?]

Basketball Classics:

Wilt the Stilt (Wilt Chamberlain)

Dr. J (Julius Erving)

Magic Johnson

Pistol Pete Maravich

Larry Legend (Larry Bird)

Air Jordan

Hakeem the Dream Olajuwon

Personal favorites:

The Mailman (Karl Malone)

The Ice Man (George Gervin)

Clyde the Glide Drexler

The Stifle Tower (Rudy Gobert)

Chocolate Thunder (Darryl Dawkins)

AK-47 (Andrei Kirilenko)

The Greek Freak (Giannis Antetokounmpo)

[Since Robbie Rankin grew up a Rangers fan, I'm providing you
with a bonus.]

Hockey Classics:

Mr. Hockey (Gordie Howe)

Rocket Richard

Boom Boom Geoffrion

The Golden Jet (Bobby Hull)

The Great One (Wayne Gretzky)

The Great Eight (Alexander Ovechkin)

Sid the Kid Crosby

Personal favorites:

Alf the Embalmer Pike

Wally the Whirling Dervish Stanowski

Rod the Secretary of Defense Langway

Pat Little Ball of Hate Verbeek

Stu the Grim Reaper Grimson

Wayne the Intimidator Belak

Derek the Boogie Man Boogaard

After a delicious meal, they put the kid to bed, and the three of us sat in the living room (they held hands), and we talked about all kinds of stuff. Canon law, the canonization case, more sports (Ronnie had been a track star in high school), their plans to spend Valentine's Day in Rome, the death of Ronnie's father last year, my failed marriage (briefly), etc.

Everything under the sun except my problem.

Which wasn't Robbie's fault since neither of us knew what the hell I was doing in his living room, except for the fact that the alleged "saint" in the stone tower had willed it into being.

"It must be nice," Ronnie said, "to live in New Jersey and know that he's up there."

When I didn't get her meaning, which was obvious to her husband, she explained.

"Because he's up there praying, which means he must be up there praying for you, Richard."

I hadn't considered it.

"Maybe he is," I admitted.

Eventually, I felt that I was overstaying, so I stood up.

It was almost ten o'clock.

"I should be getting home."

"Why not spend the night here?" Ronnie offered.

"Thanks, but I really need to hit the road."

I thanked them for a lovely evening, and they told me to come back anytime.

"Or call," Robbie added.

At the door, after I'd shaken hands with Robbie, Ronnie hugged me close.

"The whole air about us," she whispered, "is filled with angels."

Which seemed both weird as hell and perfectly appropriate. Later in my hotel room at the airport, I googled the quote. It was from some saint named John Chrysostom, who was an early church father and the archbishop of Constantinople in the Fourth Century.

When the door shut behind me, I looked out at the Chesapeake again. Dark, black, mysterious, dangerous, and beautiful in the moonlight.

Behind me, the little family was snug in their little cottage. Happy, in love, with one amazing child, with another on the way.

Maybe that's why I'd been sent to coastal Maryland?

To get a glimpse of how it's done.

Chapter 23

Woodlawn Cemetery

(Sunday, 1/23/22)

The Lord Is My Shepherd

S imple.

Engraved on a simple headstone.

I was standing over the fresh grave of the kid who'd nearly killed me in front of Madison Square Garden six weeks ago. It seemed most likely that the kid had saved my life by swerving at the last minute when his black van went out of control.

Maybe.

Probably.

The family, originally from the Bronx, had decided to bury the kid in Woodlawn Cemetery, located somewhere on the graveyard's four hundred acres on Woodlawn Heights. When I arrived at the cemetery gate, it was open, but the gatehouse itself was closed on Sunday. Fortunately, there were maps and brochures left for Sunday visitors in a wall file attached to the front door.

Woodlawn Cemetery, it seems, is one of the most famous graveyards in the entire country.

Full of the well-known dead.

Herman Melville
Bat Masterson (!)
Irving Berlin
Nellie Bly
R. H. Macy
Celia Cruz
Dorothy Parker
Damon Runyon
Countee Cullen
George M. Cohan
F.W. Woolworth
Duke Ellington
And many others

Ironically (I suppose), also Grantland Rice.

"The Dean of Sportswriters."

Who died back in 1954 after many years at the *New York Tribune*, who was the most famous sportswriter in the country, who covered and generally acclaimed the likes of Jim Thorpe, Babe Ruth, Jack Dempsey, Bobby Jones, Knute Rockne, and many others.

His elevated poetic style was a bit over the top for me, but I read a million of his old syndicated columns when I was a teenager, and I've always respected the man for what he did for sportswriting in general.

He made it a respected vocation.

He also made it mandatory reading.

Intrigued, I followed the cemetery map and found Rice's small flat marker and paid my respects.

With a prayer.

It was a chilly, windy, overcast day, and it was getting late in the afternoon, gradually getting darker.

It was time to find young Carlos Molina.

Fortunately, yesterday morning, I'd called the gatehouse and asked where the kid was buried.

"He's in Section 23," a pleasant young woman told me.

"Will I be able to find it?"

"Yes, he's not far from Herman Melville."

So I used my map again and tracked down the great novelist. Had I ever read *Moby-Dick*? No, of course not. I don't read novels (even though, at the moment, I'm actually writing some kind of memoir supposedly in a novelistic style, whatever that means), so why would I use the word "great"?

Because my old man once told me that *Moby-Dick* was the greatest novel that he'd ever read (and he'd read a ton), and he also told me that I should read the book as soon as possible. He even bought me my own copy. That was way back when I was a junior in high school, and I still haven't gotten around to it.

Maybe it was time to do what my father suggested.

Anyway, I eventually found Herman Melville's gravestone, which had some kind of writer's scroll engraved into his tombstone above his name, and I assured the old boy that I'd make the time to read his book soon.

Then I looked around in the twilight, wondering how big Section 23 might be. I guess I'd have to check out every grave, but at least I could focus on the newer markers.

It started to rain.

Lightly.

Off to my right, within hilly Section 23, I saw an umbrella open, so I headed in that general direction. It was a small attractive Hispanic woman, maybe thirty-five or so, standing over a newish gray tombstone.

The Lord Is My Shepherd
Carlos Juan Molina
2004-2021
The Light of our Lives

She was wearing a dark trench coat.

She turned around when she heard me approaching, and I could see that she'd been crying in the rain.

I tried to put her mind at ease.

"I've come to pay my respects," I assured her.

She didn't seem displeased.

She looked down at the grave and nodded.

"He was such a good boy," she said, trying to keep her composure.

Naturally, I didn't know what I should say.

"Are you family?" I tried.

"I am. I'm his aunt Isabel."

She left it right there, so we stood in the silence for a bit. With Isabel standing under her little umbrella. With me standing impervious to the light rain.

"He was coming to get me that night," she said softly. "I was working at Bloomingdale's in lower Manhattan, and Carlos offered to pick me up. When I told him that I could take the subway, he insisted, and now he's dead."

"It's not your fault," I said stupidly, but she didn't seem offended.

"I know that, and I've accepted it, but it's still a fact that he'd be alive today if I hadn't agreed to let him drive down and pick me up."

She clearly needed to change the subject.

She looked at me directly.

"How did you know Carlos? Were you one of his EMT teachers?"

"No."

It seemed as though the young kid wanted to be an EMT, and the last time I saw him they were loading his stretcher into an EMT van on Seventh Avenue.

It was obvious that his aunt wanted more, so I told her the truth.

"I was there the night that Carlos died outside the Garden."

She was astonished.

"I think he saved my life," I continued. "When the van went out of control, he was racing right towards me, but then the van swerved at the last minute. I'd be dead otherwise."

To be honest, I had no idea what had *really* happened, but it certainly *might* have happened that way.

Overwhelmed, Isabel began to cry. She lowered her umbrella, leaned into me, and rested her head on my chest. I held her gently.

Eventually, when she got control of herself again, she stepped back and lifted up her umbrella again.

"Thank you for telling me that," she said.

I tried to explain myself further.

"I've been wanting to come here and say a prayer for him. Earlier today, I lit some candles at Tolentine."

St. Nicholas of Tolentine.

The Cathedral of the Bronx.

She nodded gratefully.

"What was he like?" I wondered. "The obituaries made him sound like a saint. Honor student, athlete, college scholarship, and all the rest of it."

She smiled.

"It's all true. He was a special kid. He kept himself away from the drugs and the gangs, but he was still a young boy. He could be foolish sometimes, and very headstrong, and he didn't always listen to my sister, his mother."

"There are worse things."

"Yes, there are. CJ was determined to help people in this messed-up world. Years ago, his grandfather had died in a terrible car crash on the Cross Bronx Expressway, and Carlos made up his mind to be a medic. He wanted to help crash victims, then he ended up one himself."

"Well, he certainly did me a lot of good," I pointed out. "I think he saved my life."

Isabel nodded again, then looked up at me directly and pointed at the headstone.

"He really was 'The Light of our Lives.'"

"That's a much better legacy than most."

"Yes, it is."

But now, of course, his light had been extinguished.

Chapter 24

Connick

(Thursday, 2/4/22)

He kicked off the next song.

Gently, melodically.

Why do stars fall down from the sky
Every time you walk by?

It was his cover of the old Carpenters' song.

"Close to You."

Which I guess, at the moment, was rather ironic.

Earlier today, I was feeling worn out with St. Francis and *Moby-Dick,* so on the spur of the moment, I hopped in my Range Rover Sport, drove down to Red Bank, and bought a ticket to see Harry Connick, Jr., at the Basie tonight.

Which was the same concert that I'd been planning to take Katie to see as an early Valentine's Day present.

It was a lousy seat, way in the back, which was fine with me. I could still see Cindy sitting up front in the second row from the stage next to her older sister Melanie, who never really approved of me.

Maybe with good reason.

Regardless, Melanie seemed quite comfortable taking advantage of the Connick tickets that I'd sent to Cindy in the mail. Anonymously. Did they suspect that the tickets came from me? Most probably, but who knows? Besides, what difference would it have made? We're talking about Harry Connick, Jr., right?

By the way, what's the deal with this guy?

Sure, I get how talented he is. A great singer, a great musician, a likeable actor, charming as hell, and all the rest of it. But why does he make almost every adult woman weak in the knees? To some extent, I can understand Brad Pitt, George Clooney, and Mark Wahlberg. But the Sinatra crooner from New Orleans? Sure he's a nice-looking guy, but there's something else about him that gets women fired up.

Something hard to define.

Especially for a male like me.

Whatever the reasons, every single female that I know would put him in her top five. Katie, Cindy, Rebeka, Melanie, Lili, etc. All of them. Maybe the fact that he was a practicing Catholic who loved his wife and three daughters gave him extra cred with the women in my life. When Covid kicked off, he got especially serious about serious things and produced an album called *Alone with My Faith* in 2021, singing songs like "Amazing Grace" and "How Great Thou Art." On the more secular side of things, I've probably watched *Hope Floats* at least five times with Katie, and, yeah, I enjoyed the romance, and I enjoyed Harry and Sandra Bullock, but I still don't fully understand the extent of the Connick fascination.

Oh, well, I guess I never will. There's obviously something that I don't understand about the female psyche, if "psyche" is the appropriate word.

At the moment, he was currently singing the hell out of the Carpenters' song.

Just like me, they long to be
Close to you.

I looked around the Basie. It's a handsome classic theater that first opened back in 1926 as the Carleton Theater and was renamed in 1984 for jazz great Count Basie, a Red Bank native. I've been here a few times before (Tony Bennett, Darlene Love, Olivia Newton-John) with the various females in my life, and I remember one curious piece of trivia about the place. When it first opened in 1926, it featured a silent film starring some guy named Richard Dix in a film called *The Quarterback*.

Sports haunts me everywhere.

Even back before I was born.

There's no escape.

So, yes, I admit it, I was stalking Cindy again. Listening to Harry, but staring long-distance at the back of my ex-wife's head.

Like an idiot.

Remembering the day it all ended.

I'd been off in Arlington, Texas, for the highly anticipated Manny Pacquiao beatdown of Antonio Margarito inside the huge "Jerry

World" (Cowboys Stadium) for the WBC super welterweight title. After the fight, I ran into Evander Holyfield, and we set up an interview for the following afternoon. When our meeting got postponed until Monday, I ended up spending a few more days than originally planned in Texas.

After all, what sportswriter in his right mind wouldn't want to sit down and talk with Evander Holyfield?

So I texted my wife.

Delayed in Dallas. Love.

Which I guess, like a lot of other stuff in my life back then, was entirely inadequate.

When I got back to New Jersey, I drove down to the Sea Girt cottage to meet with Cindy.

She was out back.

On the beach.

She turned around and didn't waste time.

"I've had enough, Richie."

I didn't realize how serious it was.

"I'm sorry, Cindy, but it was a great opportunity."

"It's not about Dallas, Richie."

I was confused.

"Then what's it about?"

"It's about us. It's not working, and I'm leaving."

I was stunned.

With hindsight, I shouldn't have been stunned, but I was.

She explained in a single sentence.

"A marriage that puts sports, or anything else, above children isn't really a marriage."

A few months earlier, I'd told her that I didn't want children. At least, not yet. Afterwards, whenever she brought up the subject, I refused to talk about it, then I'd go off somewhere and bury myself in sports.

What else?

I suppose that moment on the beach was the moment when I should have said something like, "Well, Cindy, let's talk about it some more." Or better yet, "Maybe I can try and reconsider things, Cindy."

But in truth, I didn't want to reconsider anything.

I was at the top, or very near the top, of the sportswriting hierarchy, and I didn't want to be distracted by anything else.

So I stood there on the hard November sand completely bewildered.

"What are you talking about, Cindy?"

"I'm leaving you," she repeated.

"Divorce?" I said still mystified. After all, Cindy was a serious Catholic, and we'd only been married for about twelve months.

"Separated, Richie," she clarified. "For now, I'm going home to my parents. You need to think about things and get your priorities straight."

Then she gave me a quick cold kiss on the cheek and walked back to the beach house.

Stunned, angry as hell, I watched her go.

I was too busy feeling sorry for myself, and too busy imagining myself as the injured party, to realize what I had done. That I'd been relegating the one I loved to a distant second place behind my sports obsession.

She was wearing her red L.L. Bean hooded mountain jacket, which she loved, which I also loved, and black jeans and boots.

I can still see her walking away from me.

Later, when my mind drifted back to the concert, Harry was singing a song that was probably titled "Only You."

When you hold my hand, I understand the magic that you do,
You're my dream come true, my one and only you.

Yeah.

I wondered if I should accidentally bump into Cindy after the concert and say hello.

To say something.

To say anything.

But I didn't.

Instead, I left during the encores.

Chapter 25

Palm Beach

(Sunday, 3/20/22)

I was on the edge of my seat.

I know that sounds ridiculous, but I was literally sitting on the front edge of my seat.

It was the eighth inning, and the Nationals were losing to the despicable Astros 2-1.

Chad Donato walked Jackson Cluff.

Jacob Young singled as Cluff moved to third.

Lucius Fox pinch hit a double to right center as Cluff scored and Young moved to third.

2-2.

Then Darren Baker hit a sacrifice to center, and Young scored.

3-2.

I'm not much for exuberant cheering, but I was doing so within my heart.

It felt marvelous.

Like an addiction gratified.

Which, I guess, reinforces the addiction concept since the game was totally meaningless, and most of the players (except for Juan Soto and Nelson Cruz) were people that very few baseball fans could have identified.

Mostly young prospects.

But it was still baseball.

And it was a victory over the hated Astros. The team that had cheated its way to the 2017 World Series title and robbed Aaron Judge of that year's MVP because its batters were stealing signs with a camera in the outfield then relaying upcoming pitches into the clubhouse, where they were signaled to the Astros' batters by banging a garbage can in the dugout.

Yes, a garbage can.

Sometimes whistling, sometimes blinking outfield lights, but mostly banging on a trash can, which you can clearly hear on the YouTube clips.

It was a disgrace.

Just ask any MLB hitter about how much difference it makes knowing what pitch is coming next.

Eventually, the team got caught, there was a B.S. investigation, and the players admitted what they'd done. Which sounds simple enough, right? Naturally, the commissioner (Rob Manfred) would suspend all the players for at least a year or two and then make restitutions in the record books.

Right?

Hardly, the players were given immunity for their testimony (confessions), and they were *entirely* unpunished. Only the manager (A. J. Hinch) and the general manager (Jeff Luhnow) were suspended for a year, and the team was forced to forfeit a few draft picks (big deal) and fined five million dollars (peanuts).

All the other players as well as the fans were outraged.

Mike Trout was clear about it.

They cheated. I don't agree with the punishments, the players not getting anything. It was a player-driven thing.

Aaron Judge demanded that the Astros World Series title be vacated, and home run legend Hank Aaron was even more blunt.

I think whoever did that should be out of baseball for the rest of their lives.

As already mentioned, I was so angry about the scandal that I was planning to write a book about it, but I eventually decided against it. I knew that other capable writers would write their own exposés, and I felt that I'd already vented so much spleen in *Roids* about the steroids/PED scandal that maybe I should leave this one alone.

Which I did.

But I was glad to see that the Astros were mercilessly booed as cheaters when the 2019 season got underway, as the fans, except those blindly loyal in Houston, never forgot about what they'd done.

So I'd been rooting against them ever since, especially enjoying their loss to the Nationals in the 2019 World Series. Even today, down here in sunny Florida for a meaningless Spring Training game in half-filled but beautiful Palm Beach Ballpark, I greatly enjoyed seeing them lose. Even though the main Astro culprits (Altuve, Bregman, etc.) weren't even playing today, with the exception of Carlos Correa, who was appropriately booed during each of his plate appearances.

Good.

And it was especially good that the Nationals closed out the game with some good pitching, winning 3-2.

Yet totally insignificant.

Thus unlike (sportswise) the Super Bowl a month ago where the Rams (thankfully) beat the self-important Bengals. (Unless, as I sometimes believe, *all* sports is meaningless.)

Certainly not like the truly horrific Russian invasion into Ukraine a few weeks ago.

Or the terrible airstrike on the Mariupol Theatre that killed six hundred Ukrainian citizens four days ago.

Or even, on a more personal level, my own readings of the *Philothea* and Melville's amazing *Whale*. After all, hasn't everyone, at some point in his life, felt like Ishmael floundering around in the churning sea clinging to Queequeg's coffin?

I was then, but slowly, drawn towards the closing vortex.

But not today.

I was enjoying myself.

What's more glorious than baseball in the spring?

But why, you might ask, was I down here in Palm Beach, avoiding all the reporters, watching a meaningless game in the Grapefruit League?

I had a motive.

A purpose.

I wasn't down here on some kind of assignment, I was down here because I had business of my own to attend to.

Earlier, from my isolated seat high in Section 116, I'd spotted her sitting down below in the boxes right behind the Nationals' dugout. I knew that she was here in Palm Beach because I'd been reading her columns in the *Washington Post*, aware that she'd been sent down to Florida to cover the Nationals' spring training. I was also aware that she was down here with her mom and her little boy Eddie, both of whom she'd briefly referenced in her spring training reports online.

As Cade Cavalli struck out the Astros' Chad Stevens for the final out, I came up behind her. She was sitting in her seat, typing a few notes on her little laptop.

Sitting next to her was an older woman holding a young sleeping child.

A child less than a year old.

As I'd expected.

As I'd hoped.

When Irene sensed me standing behind her, she turned her head.

She'd been ghosting me for three months, but she didn't seem surprised to see me.

She wasted no time.

"He's *not* yours, Ritchie. I told you that."

I must admit she looked lovely as hell. Tight jeans (not too tight), light yellow windbreaker, and a Nationals baseball cap.

Who doesn't love a girl in a baseball cap?

Cap or not, it was easy to see why she could easily attract any man she wanted.

Including me.

"You're a liar, Irene," I pointed out matter-of-factly.

The older woman, realizing that things might get ugly, looked over at Irene.

"I'll let you two deal with each other, Irene," she said. "I'm taking Eddie out to the car."

I felt bad about ruining her day, so I looked at the older woman directly.

"I'm sorry about this," I said.

She could see that I was sincere.

"I understand. I really do. Irene's told me what she's done, and how she's misled you."

Which I thought was especially magnanimous. I guess raising Irene as a daughter was no walk in the park.

"Can I see the boy?" I asked.

Little Eddie was still sleeping, held against his grandmother's breast. She turned a bit so I could see his face.

Like the older Rankin kid in Maryland, he was adorable. Even asleep, even with his eyes shut. With dark hair and a sweet child's face.

"He looks like me," I said to both women.

"But he's not yours, Richie," the grandmother assured me, "but I'll let Irene try and convince you."

Then I watched her walk away, up the aisle, carrying a little child that might or might not have been my own.

I turned back to Irene.

"Go ahead, tell me some more lies."

"You're right, Richie, I *am* a liar sometimes," she admitted, "but not about this. Eddie's definitely his and not yours."

I assumed "his" meant her husband Benjamin Beckett, whom she supposedly couldn't stand.

"So everything's just fine in Great Falls, I guess," I said sarcastically.

"No, Richie, nothing's fine, but at least we're no longer together."

"Why?"

"Lots of reasons, but the last straw was because the idiot convinced himself that Eddie is someone else's child."

"Mine?"

"No, of course not."

Which naturally made me wonder how many other men like me there'd been in her life.

In her married life.

"Were there many?" I asked.

Meaning, were there many other occasional lovers like me.

She didn't answer, which was an answer itself.

Apparently, I was just one of many, or at least one of a few.

Or was she lying again?

"Look, Richie, you have to understand that our marriage was a total mess long before I got pregnant and long before Benjamin went to that medical conference in Cancun. He was discontent with every-thing, and he was impossible to live with. Nasty and belligerent. He'd become a terrible insomniac, roaming about the house all night long and accusing me of all kinds of stuff during the days when he wasn't working at the hospital. Accusing me of stuff that I didn't even do."

"Then why did you tell me that the boy was mine?"

"I've already told you, Richie! I was drunk that night, and I was all alone, and Eddie was asleep, and my marriage was crashing. So I sent you a text and wrote what I wished was actually true."

Which surprised me.

"You wished that Eddie was mine?"

"Of course, you idiot, it would have been much better than the truth. That I was stuck with Ben in a hopelessly loveless marriage."

"What happens now?"

She shrugged.

"Who knows? I'm down here living with my mom in Lauderdale. I guess I'm on my own."

I thought things over.

"I'm not sure that I can believe you, Irene."

"About what?"

"About whether I'm the father or not."

She shook her head wearily.

"You're definitely not, Richie," she repeated, "but I wish you were."

I couldn't imagine why she would wish such a thing, but I suppose anybody seemed better than her husband.

Regardless, I still didn't know what I believed and what I didn't.

About anything.

Irene stood up from her seat, looking beautiful, looking out at the field.

"There's nothing like baseball, Richie," she said wistfully.

"And nothing better than beating the damned Astros."

"Damned right about that!"

She looked at me intently.

Maybe even seductively.

"Why don't you take me to dinner tonight?"

At that moment, it occurred to me that she might be out of her mind.

"I don't think so, Irene."

She shrugged once again.

"Oh, well," she said, as she walked away.

Mysterious and lovely as ever.

Chapter 26

Copacabana

(Tuesday, 3/22/22)

I walked up the tiled promenade.

With the ocean and the beach to my left.

The most famous beach in the world.

I won't attempt to describe Copacabana since you've surely seen pictures of the place before your eyes went dark. Or maybe you were down there yourself at some point. As for me, I'll just say that no picture could ever do it justice.

It was a sunny lively afternoon in Rio, and the crescent-shaped beach was appropriately crowded, as were all the nearby shops, cafes, boutiques, restaurants, and hotels.

I was heading north in the direction of the distant Fort Duque de Caxias, built by the Portuguese in 1779, walking over the Promenade's black and white Portuguese tiles, which were set in some kind of curious wave pattern.

I briefly remembered being on the beach six years ago thinking about a beautiful Carioca while I was watching the bronze medal game (women's beach volleyball) in the brand-new Arena de Vôlei de Praia during the 2016 Olympic Games. Which was won by the Americans (April Ross and Kerri Walsh-Jennings) over the two Brazilian semifinalists.

Go Yanks!

Then I pushed it out of my mind and entered the florist shop.

Flores Celestiais.

The scent engulfed me.

Marvelously.

The owner was preparing an arrangement at a table behind the counter.

With her back to me.

I wondered if it was Inês.

She turned around to wait on me.

I'd flown down to Florida to try and resolve the Irene business (without complete satisfaction), and now I'd flown from Miami down to Rio to resolve the Inês business.

Did my father really have a South American lover?

Everyone who knew my old man would have scoffed at the idea. Including me. But I still felt compelled to understand the mysterious text that I'd received after the deadly accident in front of Madison Square Garden. I also needed to get to the bottom of the Inês email sent to my father back in 1966, which was signed "Love, always, Inês."

What did it mean?

I'd texted back to the text, of course, but I was ghosted.

Then I tried emailing Inês from my father's old computer.

Nothing.

So I had Mack Dawson track down the source of the text from three months ago.

Oddly enough, it had not been sent from Caracas, but from a florist shop in Rio, which made things even more confusing.

Rather than call the florist shop on the phone and get the runaround, I decided to come down here in person.

I needed to resolve this.

As mentioned, she turned around.

Naturally, I couldn't believe what I was seeing.

I was stunned!

And she, of course, was stunning as well.

A tight white dress to her knees, long black thick Brazilian hair, intense dark Portuguese eyes, and a warm and perfect tropical smile.

Looking like a model.

Whom I'd not only met before, but actually slept with.

Right here in Rio!

It would be hard to say who was more shocked. I guess it was me, but it was definitely close.

"Richard?" she said.

"Joana?" I said.

I met her six years ago when I was covering the Rio Olympics for *Sports Illustrated* (mostly boxing and track). She bumped into me at a concessions stand in João Havelange Stadium, and we started talking. Kidding around. Since I'd spilled her drink, I offered to buy her another one after the 100-meter finals. When she said yes in her killer Carioca accent, we agreed to meet back at the concession stand.

Back in my seat, I watched as Usain Bolt (the "Human Lightning Bolt") won the 100 meters, as he would also win the 200 meters a few days later, as he would also lead the Jamaican 4/100 team to gold the day after that. On the day that I met Joana (August 14), Bolt became the first man to win three consecutive Olympic golds in the 100 meters (2008 in Beijing, 2012 in London, and now 2016 in Rio). It was truly amazing, and I felt very fortunate to be there (and get an interview with Bolt two days later), but I have to admit, it was hard to concentrate on track after meeting Joana.

Impossible.

Later, after some more kidding around, I took her to eat at Pérgula, a popular restaurant in the Copacabana Palace where I was staying. In truth, the Palace was far too ritzy for a Jersey Rutgers guy, having been built for the Rio visit of the Belgium King Albert back in 1920, but it was pre-assigned and paid for by *Sports Illustrated*.

Joana and I hit it off.

Immediately.

Connected somehow.

She was a realtor from Ipanema who'd run track when she was a young girl, and she was determined, regardless of the cost, to see as many of the track stars and track events at the Olympics as possible, especially Usain Bolt, Allyson Felix, the American women 110 hurdles team, and Brazil's own Thiago Braz da Silva, who won gold in the pole vault. She was also determined to see the final futebol matches, which were eventually won by Brazil and their superstar Neymar.

At the Pérgula, we drank way too many Caipirinhas (cachaça, lime juice, sugar), and we ended up in my suite on the twentieth floor overlooking the ocean.

I don't know *how* it happened, and I won't attempt to describe *what* happened.

When I woke up the next morning, Joana was gone. It was as if it had never happened. As if she wasn't really real, even though the scent of her still lingered in the room. Naturally, I looked for her at all the subsequent track competitions at the stadium, and I found myself distracted by thoughts of her throughout the rest of the amazing Olympics. Despite all the early concerns about Rio hosting the Olympics, especially those unpleasant rumors about "superbacteria," favela gangs, and unfinished venues, the Olympics was amazing, historic, and unforgettable.

It was the Olympics not only of Bolt and Neymar, but of Katie Ledecky, Michael Phelps, Carmelo and the US basketball team, etc. Brazil had its best Olympics ever, and the US dominated overall with 121 medals, 46 gold.

But for me personally, Joana was still on my mind during the long flight home.

And afterwards as well.

What *was* that all about anyway?

I had no idea.

She was lovely, and she was a serious Catholic. So what was she doing in my bed at the Palace?

Back in New Jersey, I mentioned what had happened in the confessional (admittedly doubting my "firm purpose of amendment" if I ever ran into her again) and eventually I managed to forget about her.

As best I could.

Now she was standing in front of me, amid all the colorful and fragrant flowers, looking exactly as she did six years ago.

"I'm confused," I admitted.

She understood and nodded.

"Come and sit with me," she said.

Then she led me over to a small table with two chairs, and we sat facing each other. There was a book and red flowers on the table.

"I'm the daughter of Inês Peres. Do you know who she was, Richard?"

I realized that I'd never actually known Joana's last name. Which didn't seem very important at the time.

"Yes, I believe she was a young girl whom my father sponsored many years ago, and whom he seems to have met when she was older."

"Yes, when she was twenty."

She explained.

Inês Peres was born extremely poor and illegitimate in Rochinha, one of the largest favelas in Rio. When she was ten, she was sponsored by my old man through the Christian Foundation for Children, which allowed young Inês and her mother to move out of the favela.

"My mother always believed that Dr. Ramsey had saved her life, which I believe as well."

"So what happened in New York?"

"When my mother was fifteen, she began working in a small florist shop in Ipanema. By the time she was nineteen, she'd managed to open this little shop right here on the beach. Being so well-located, it was very successful, and my mother saved her money so she could go to New York and meet your father."

"What happened?"

She seemed surprised by the question.

"She thanked him of course."

Then she apprehended my suspicions.

"Oh, no, Richard," she laughed, "it was nothing like that! Your father was much older and a perfect gentleman."

"Well, an email that I found on his computer after he died seemed to indicate otherwise."

I showed her the email.

Yes, it was the best night of my life. Love, always, Inês

Joana read it and laughed again.

It was a lovely laugh.

"Yes, it *was* the best night of her life, silly boy! She'd finally met the man who'd saved her from poverty and from who knows what else?"

"But she signed it 'Love, always'?" I tried.

She smiled at my foolishness.

"Brazilian women can be *very* passionate, Richard. You should know all about that. Besides, her English was never really that good."

All right, fine, so my father wasn't a cheating bastard. To be honest, it was quite a relief, but it was hardly the end of the story.

"So what about this?"

I showed her the text that I'd received outside Madison Square Garden three months ago.

Meu Amor – I'll be in New York next week before returning to Caracas. Can we meet again? Love, Inês

Joana got serious.

Thoughtful.

"Yes, Richie, my mother was dying of brain cancer at the time. It affected her behavior, and sometimes she was deliriously sick. One afternoon, she sent that message from here at the florist shop. She'd Googled "Richard Ramsey," got a hold of your phone number, then texted what she texted. She was out of her mind at the time, Richard, and had apparently reverted back into her past."

"Why Caracas?"

"Because her cousin had made an appointment with some bigtime oncologist in Venezuela, but my mother's cancer was too far advanced, so we never went. She died a few weeks after she'd sent you that text."

"I'm sorry, Joana."

But I was still curious.

"Why do you think I only found that one email in my father's computer?"

"I know why."

Which obviously saddened her, so I waited patiently.

"Soon after my mother returned to Rio from New York, she got pregnant with me, and her boyfriend abandoned her. My mom was devastated, and she didn't want your father to know about it, but she also didn't want to lie about it, so she cut off their correspondence. It bothered her for the rest of her life. She was ashamed, Richard, which is something I know something about."

Which seemed to be the right time to bring up six years ago.

"So what about the Olympics? And what about Joana, the realtor? Hell, is Joana even your real name?"

"It is."

This was obviously hard for her, but she did her best, clearly fighting off the urge to cry as she was explaining.

"My mother and I followed your father's career, and your mother's career as well, as best we could down here in Brazil, and we did the same thing with you. I also grew up loving sports, and I was extremely impressed that you'd become a famous sportswriter. Six years ago when I was eighteen, I discovered that you were coming to the Olympics for *Sports Illustrated*, and I made up my mind to find you at the track events. It wasn't very hard."

She pointed to my left eye.

Meaning my eye patch.

"Yeah," I agreed, "it's a bit distinctive."

She smiled and continued.

"All I wanted to do was thank you for everything that your family had done for my mother, but I was still feeling a bit awkward about it, so I decided to bump into you on purpose and play it by ear. I certainly had no intention of doing what I did. What *we* did."

We were both silent for a moment in the flower room.

"There was an attraction," she admitted. "Right from the first moment. It was very powerful."

"Yes, for me too."

"So I did what I shouldn't have done, and I didn't tell you who I really was, or why I'd tracked you down. I even lied to you and told you that I was a realtor. I have no idea where that came from. I was young and stupid and suddenly infatuated."

It seemed as though she was talking to herself.

Then she looked over at me directly.

"I don't tell lies, Richard. And I've never done anything like what happened that night, either before or since. Afterwards, I was terribly ashamed of myself, and I snuck away and went home, and I never told my mother anything about it. Instead, I went to see my priest, and I confessed myself, and he told me to pray for you. Which helped me deal with it. So I've prayed for you ever since. Every single night."

It was hard to comprehend that my selfish behavior six years ago had led to so many prayers. I didn't know what to say.

"I'm sorry," I said stupidly, but I meant it.

Then she tapped the book on the table.

"This also helped a lot."

I turned it over and read the cover.

Introducción a la Vida Devota.

St. Francis De Sales!

Again!

I couldn't help but ask.

"Why this particular book?"

She thought it was an odd question.

She shrugged.

"My priest, who's a grumpy old Jesuit, suggested it. After all, it's one of the most popular books in Christendom."

"When did he suggest it?"

"Six years ago. After you-know-what."

Meaning our night at Copacabana Palace.

Then she reached over the small table and took my hand.

"What about you, Richard? Have you found somebody?"

If you're wondering, old man Jesuit, if I was wondering if all this might have been romantically predestined somehow, it definitely flit through my curious mind.

Was it possible that we were oddly destined for each other?

"No," I said, although I was fully aware that I'd surely found my "somebody" then lost her twelve years ago on the beach behind my cottage in Sea Girt.

Then a silent guy quietly approached from the back room behind the counter. He was a nice-looking Carioca, short like Joana, and dressed in beach pastels.

He came over to our table.

When Joana stood up, I did the same.

"This is Richard Dawson, *querido*. It was his father who helped out Inês when she was a child."

He obviously knew the story.

She turned to me.

"And this is Rafael, my fiancé," she said proudly.

We shook hands.

"Nice to be meeting you," he said with a smile, in an English that was much clunkier than Joana's.

"Will you stay at Rio?" he asked. "You could stay for dinner with us."

"Thanks, Rafael, but I'm leaving tonight," I explained, which was close to the truth. My flight was scheduled for 9:15 tomorrow morning."

"Well, I wish you well," he said with another smile.

Then he said something to Joana in Portuguese, and I caught the word *flores*. When she answered, he nodded politely to both of us and returned to the back room.

Joana looked over at me.

"I've been very blessed," she said.

Even though I'd only seen the guy for two minutes, it was obvious that he worshipped the ground she walked on.

Why wouldn't he?

Joana leaned into me and kissed me on the cheek.

"I pray for you every day," she whispered.

"I hope so, Joana."

Then I left her paradise of tropical flowers and exited onto the glaring hot mosaic promenade of Copacabana.

Chapter 27

Mike Trout Field

(Monday, 4/11/22)

S ame seats, same field, but a different name.

After batting .326 and hitting thirty home runs in his first full season with the California Angels, Mike Trout was selected Rookie of the Year. Always grateful to his high school alma mater, the Millville Thunderbolts, he donated his bonus for winning the award to Millville Senior High, and they renamed their upgraded baseball field in his honor.

Mike Trout Field.

Which is where I was sitting, watching the baseball team warm-up, getting ready for today's conference game against Egg Harbor Township.

Fourteen years ago, I'd met her right here, sitting where I was right now.

But what was I doing here today?

When I was a kid and told my father that I wanted to be a sports-writer, he told me to always pay attention to high school sports. It's what all the local news outlets have to cover, and it's also where all the college and MLB players come from.

"Don't ever be a snob about high school sports," he'd remind me.

So I never was.

Back in 2008 during my first official year with the *Newark Star-Ledger*, I started hearing lots of buzz about this young phenom from down in the middle of nowheresville in southern New Jersey. So I started driving down to Millville, which is just southwest of the Pine Barrens and about thirty-five miles west of Atlantic City. The kid had grown up playing shortstop (since he idolized Derek Jeter even though he was a Phillies fanatic) and he pitched as well. In his senior year, he moved out to center field where he hit .531 (not a typo) and eighteen home runs, still a New Jersey state record.

By his senior year, I wasn't the only reporter making regular trips down to Millville to see the amazing "Millville Meteor."

No, I didn't give him that nickname, but I did give him lots of good press in the *Star-Ledger*, not only because he *really was* a "meteor," but because he was also a great kid whom everybody seemed to like and admire.

I'm sure you know the rest of it. After graduation, he was drafted by the Angels, did a bit in the minors, then came up to the majors and won Rookie of the Year. In the years that followed, he won three MVPs (should have won more) and was (is) generally acknowledged as the best baseball player on the planet.

No argument.

But Millville means a lot more to me than Mike Trout and Thunderbolt baseball, although, as I've told Mike a number of times, what happened was all because of him.

It was April 7, 2008.

The Thunderbolts were playing (as today) the Egg Harbor Eagles, and Mike Trout pitched an eighteen-strikeout no-hitter (also not a typo), and they won the game 6-0. I won't bother to give details or the box score since they're easy enough to look up, and I also won't bother because it's what happened pre-game during the warm-ups that changed my life. Earlier, I'd been down in the clubhouse for a quick chat with Roy Hallenbeck, the team's coach. Then I went up to the stands to get ready for the game.

But someone approached and sat next to me.

Later, when I asked her why she sat next to me, she said, "Because I *always* sit here. As a matter of fact, you're sitting in *my* seat!"

I guess I was.

Excellent move on my part.

Even before she sat down, I was hooked. I looked up as she came down the aisle, and she smiled her Cindy smile.

Cindy Sinclair never seemed to mind when people described her as the all-American girl (actually the all-American beauty), with blonde shoulder-length hair, soft blue eyes, and a ready smile and laugh.

She was carrying a Coke in one hand and a large box of Cracker Jacks in the other.

Yes, Cracker Jacks!

Which she eventually spilled all over me after Trout whiffed another hapless Eagle with a hard slider.

"Oops!"

I just smiled.

"Cracker Jacks?" I kidded.

"Of course," she smiled as well, "I'd *never* go to a game without Cracker Jacks. What would be the point?"

I was completely hooked.

Maybe mesmerized would be a better word.

As my cousin Rebeka once said, "Cindy's not only perfect for you, she's perfect period."

Cindy was a local Catholic girl from Vineland (where Trout was born). She was (is) lovely, easy-going, personable, and much smarter than me. She starred on the Thunderbolts' girl's softball team for three years, and she loved sports in general, especially the Eagles, the Phillies, and the Mets. When we met that day, she was a freshman at Princeton majoring in Classics (whatever that meant) and was planning to be a teacher. She'd had a few very short-lived boyfriends because, as her older sister Melanie once put it, "She was waiting for the right guy to come along, but then you showed up and ruined everything."

As you can see, Melanie never really cared for me. She believed that I "loved sports more than I loved people," and maybe she was right, and she warned her sister to run for the hills.

But show me a nineteen-year-old who listens to her older sister.

We had unforgettable fun that day ("fun" being another inadequate word), kidding around, laughing, and intently watching Mike blow them down one by one. An eighteen-strikeout no-hitter. Whenever things got tense, Cindy would cheer like a grammar school kid, not only because she'd once been a Thunderbolt herself, and not only because of what was happening on the diamond right in front of us, but also because her family knew the Trouts quite well, and she'd rooted for little Mikey back when he was still a kid in Little League.

Sometimes, whenever Mike would whiff some baffled Eagles hitter, with the bat still resting on his shoulder, she'd get so excited that she'd grab me and hold me tight. Then she'd realize what she was doing.

"Sorry! Sorry! I don't know what I'm doing!"

"Well, just keep doing it!" I encouraged her, and she'd laugh her unintentionally seductive laugh.

After the game, I asked for her number.

"I *never* give out my number, Mr. Sportswriter," she informed me, as if it made her sad that she wasn't capable of breaking her own rules.

So I had to work around it.

She'd already mentioned that her older sister Melanie worked as a paralegal at a small law practice in Bridgeton.

Which would surely have a website.

"Well, Cindy, since you've already made the mistake of telling me where your sister works," I suggested, "why don't I call Melanie and see if *she'll* give me your number."

Cindy seemed confused by the idea.

"She won't give you my number unless I tell her to."

"Exactly."

She understood and laughed.

That night I found Melanie's office number online, and I called her the next day.

"This is Richard Ramsey."

"Oh, yeah, the bigshot sportswriter?"

She wasn't enthusiastic.

"The little-shot sportswriter," I clarified, but it didn't help much.

"I'm only giving you her number because she told me to."

"Fine."

She gave me the number.

"You better treat her like she's the princess of the realm."

"Better."

She didn't seem convinced.

Too bad for her.

Within a year we were married.

Within another year we were divorced.

Now I sensed Cindy coming toward her seat once again.

She was carrying another Coke and Cracker Jacks, and she smiled and shook her head as if slightly amused.

"You don't look like Rebeka to me," she said.

"She told me to take her place."

Cindy shook her head again.

"I'll ring her neck."

But it was said more in exasperation than anger.

Then she sat down and looked at me directly with her serious sky-blue eyes.

"What do you want, Richie?"

She said it wearily, as if to say, "Haven't we been though this many times before?"

"I want to try again."

She went silent.

"If you're willing," I added.

Nothing.

I modified my request.

"Let me take you to the Roadhouse after the game."

Milltown's a nice southern New Jersey town, but it's definitely not the culinary capital of the world, but everybody (me included) likes to eat at the Texas Roadhouse over on Second Street. I've always liked the ribs and steaks, and Cindy especially liked the hot bread with cinnamon butter.

The Roadhouse was where we went on our first date fourteen years ago, the weekend after the Trout no-hitter.

She smiled.

"Let's just see if we make it through the game together," she decided.

"I'm good with that," I assured her.

Cindy was always killer honest, and she was making it clear just how wary she was of getting involved again.

Who could blame her?

Cindy wasn't nineteen anymore. She was now thirty-two years old and teaching Latin at Princeton Prep. She'd written a popular textbook called *Learning Latin* which was used in a lot of high schools across the country, and she'd also written *Meeting Cicero* about her favorite Latin writer. She not only loved his literary style, but she admired and agreed with his approach to life. His philosophy. His politics. His level-headedness, his optimistic humanism, his stoicism, and his ethics. For all of which he was apparently considered a "righteous pagan."

All of which was over my head.

The only Latin I knew was "alma mater" and "quid pro quo."

These days, according to Rebeka, Cindy was apparently writing a new book about the Catholic nuns who'd heroically served the wounded on Civil War battlefields.

Which I knew nothing about.

All I knew was that I wanted my wife back.

And she was, by the way, according to the Church, *still* my wife. The legal divorce had been necessary to disentangle our finances, but she never actually used the term. Just "separated." According to Rebeka, unlike me, she'd never had any serious boyfriends over the subsequent years. Just, "some guy friends," as Rebeka put it yesterday, "which is why you need to get your ass down to Millville tomorrow, find Cindy, and beg her to take you back."

"But how do I know she'll be there?" I asked.

"Because she thinks she's meeting me."

So here I was, sitting at Mike Trout Field, doing my best, but maybe I should take a moment to explain myself.

When Cindy told me she'd had enough twelve years ago, I was hurt, self-pitying, and, I guess you could say, in denial. I thought things would simply resolve themselves, but they never did. I made a few futile half-assed attempts, but since nothing had really changed in my life, Cindy said that she preferred to remain separated. In time, I made the attempt to "move on," which wasn't a very Catholic thing to do, and I knew it, but I did it anyway. So I got involved with a number of other women here and there until I met Katie Kovacs at the reception for my book *Amazin'* at Citi Field. I'm sure that I treated Katie just like I'd treated Cindy, as the second most important thing in my life, but in the beginning it really didn't matter. Throughout our two years together, I remained contentedly faithful.

Then all the "stuff" happened.

Madison Square Garden.

Katie's death.

Irene's claim about her boy Eddie.

Then my mom's death.

"Tell me the truth, Richie," Cindy asked, "are you doing this because your girlfriend died?"

"No."

"Is it because your mom died?"

I tried to be honest.

"No, I think it's because *I* nearly died."

Which was something I'd never told anyone about. Not my mom, not Rebeka, not Simon, not anyone.

Except for the two priests of course.

And Carlos's aunt in the graveyard.

Cindy was a bit taken aback.

"What are you talking about?"

So I told her.

She listened carefully.

"I'm sorry about all the things that have happened to you these past few months, Richie, but why should anything be different with us?"

"Because I've changed, Cindy. I'm being mentored by a billion-year-old priest, and he's made me read the *Philothea*."

She nodded thoughtfully.

"It's a great book. I read it after we separated."

I was amazed, but I didn't want to dwell on the book and lose my momentum.

Assuming that I had some momentum.

"It's got me praying again," I added, hoping that I wasn't using religion simply to get my wife back. But why not? It was all true.

"Let me think about it, Richie."

Which was good enough for me.

At least for now.

But there was still something else that I needed to tell her about that might blow up everything, but I needed to be honest.

"There's something else, Cindy."

"What?"

"Remember years ago when you felt that you were being stalked?"

"Of course."

"It was me."

(Note: I realize that it seems rather absurd that I once hired a private investigator to track down Cindy's stalker when the stalker was me, but I did it so that Rebeka wouldn't become suspicious that I was actually the one stalking my ex-wife. Which worked.)

I sat there waiting for a response, wondering if I'd just ruined everything, but she smiled.

"Yeah, I was always hoping that it was you," she admitted.

"Those years after you left me were hard," I tried to explain. "I guess I just wanted to feel close to you."

She didn't say anything.

"Can you forgive me, Cindy?"

"Let me think about it," she said, but this time when she said it, she was smiling.

"One more thing," I said.

Maybe I was pushing my luck.

"What now, Richie?"

"I did it again last month at the Harry Connick concert. I was sitting in the back, and it seemed like you and Melanie were having a good time up front."

"We were, Richie. I always figured it was you who'd mailed me those tickets, but Rebeka wasn't so sure about it, so I finally said the heck with it anyway. Let's face it, what female could turn down second-row seats for Harry Connick?"

She laughed at herself.

"Why didn't you say anything after the concert?" she wondered.

I shrugged, so she shrugged as well.

Then she turned to me again and looked at me very intently.

"Now, can we finally focus on baseball?"

We both understood the irony of that.

"Of course, and you can eat you bloody Cracker Jacks."

So we focused on baseball.

The Eagles beat the Thunderbolts 2-0, with runs in the second and the fifth.

Millville definitely could have used the "Millville Meteor."

But as for me, I was with my Cindy, and, in a way, it seemed just like old times.

Chapter 28

Metro Medical Associates

(Wednesday, 4/13/22)

We sat in my rental BMW and waited.

I was thinking about her kid Eddie, and she was thinking about me thinking about it.

In silence.

We were sitting across the street from the entrance to Metro Medical Associates on G Street in Washington, DC, a few blocks from the Mall.

She interrupted the unspoken subject.

"So what are you doing with yourself, Richie?"

It was a good question.

"I've been reading and rereading the *Philothea*, a book written by Francis de Sales in the early 1600s."

As would be expected, she was quite surprised.

"The saint?"

"Yeah, the saint."

"Good for you, Richie."

She didn't mean it to sound as sarcastic as it looks when I'd typed it out on the page.

But who could blame her for being a bit shocked, given my past behavior.

My immoral behavior.

So what about the book itself?

Why had the blind half-dead Jesuit up in his dark stone tower told me to read it?

Saying:

Read the Philothea, *specifically Section One, Chapters Three and Twenty-Three, and Section Three, Chapter Thirty-One.*

When I finally got around to it, I naturally started with his three "specifics."

Section One, Chapter Three is titled: "Devotion Suitable to All Kinds of Vocations and Professions."

Which seemed to get right to the heart of my problem.

There is a different practice of devotion for the gentleman and the mechanic; for the prince and the servant; for the wife, the maiden, and the widow.

All right, I guess.

I seemed to be off to a good start.

Then St. Francis reaffirmed himself more emphatically:

It is not merely an error but a heresy to suppose that a devout life is necessarily banished from the soldier's camp, the merchant's shop, the prince's court, or the domestic hearth.

Then I turned to Section One, Chapter Twenty-Three, entitled: "We Must Purify Ourselves from the Taste for Useless and Dangerous Things."

Which begins:

Sports, balls, festivities, display, the drama, in themselves are not necessarily evil things, but rather indifferent, and capable of being used or abused.

Then the saint warns that excessive attractions ("vain and idle inclinations") to such things are perilous.

. . . the heart of man, if it is encumbered with these useless attachments which are both superfluous and dangerous, cannot readily, easily, and gladly rise up to God.

Yes, I'd been using the useful word "frivolous," whereas the saint seems to prefer "useless" and "superfluous."

At least in the translation I was reading.

Regardless, it was the same deal.

The saint was talking directly to me.

Or Fr. Colt was.

Or they both were.

Lastly, I flipped further back in the book to Section Three, Chapter Thirty-One, titled: "Amusements: First, of Those Which Are Lawful."

Which is more of the same.

Air and exercise, cheerful games, music, field-sports, and the like, are such innocent amusements that they only require to be used with ordinary discretion, which confines all things to their fitting time, place, and degree.

Again, the obvious catch is the word "degree."

Meaning having an over-interest in such things.

. . . such things are as amusements, they become evils as soon as they absorb the heart.

Absorbing my heart had cost me a wife, as well as negatively affecting all the other relationships in my life. Forgive me, old man, for citing passages that you probably know by heart, but I felt that it was best to let the saint speak for himself, citing the crucial sections first published in translation by Joseph F. Wagner in 1923 and more recently reprinted by Tan Books in 2010.

Then I went back to the beginning and read the whole book through. Then I read several biographies of the saint. Apparently, he was brilliant, cultured, kindly, eloquent, witty, and, to top it all off, handsome as well. For four long years, he wandered around the Chablis mountains re-converting about seventy thousand Calvinist heretics back to the Catholic Church. In doing so, he used the novel method of handing out broadsheets (like leaflets or handbills) to reaffirm his theological positions. It was for this reason, along with his many other writings, including *An Introduction to the Devout Life*, that Pius XI declared him the patron saint of writers and journalists in 1923.

The *Philothea* was a highly unusual devotional in its time since it was addressed to ordinary Catholics and not just to priests and other clerics. Francis believed that piety wasn't only reserved for members of the clergy, but that anyone, if willing, could lead a devout (thus contented) life regardless of one's station in life.

Or one's occupation.

Which, although he didn't say it in so many words, would include sportswriters.

The problem, as in my case, of course, was that I'd made sports into an all-consuming false idol, putting it before God and putting it before my loved ones as well.

Both the saint and the old man in the tower seemed to be saying to me that yes, sports is just an entertainment, but someone involved with sports can do so appropriately if he keeps his priorities straight.

Yes, sports *are* frivolous, but sports are also acceptable, unless they become dangerous.

Fine.

It was clear that I needed to readjust my life as well as my thinking, and I believe that I've done so.

Or at least, as I told Cindy, the process was underway.

Now back to Irene's reasonable question in my rented BMW.

"I've been thinking about Gil Hodges," I explained.

"A book?"

"Yeah, a bio."

"I think that's a great idea."

She meant it.

"I'm also," I added, "trying to get back with my wife. If she'll have me."

She nodded thoughtfully.

"That sounds good too, Richie. I'm sorry if I messed things up."

"No, Irene, I'd messed up things long before we ever ran into each other."

She was obviously relieved.

Then we spotted activity across the street.

Alerted, we watched intently as Dr. Benjamin Beckett, Irene's husband, was escorted from the offices of Metro Medical Associates, where he was a highly regarded neurologist. He was wearing handcuffs and seemingly expressionless, as he was ushered into a DC police van under the careful watch of several DC detectives and two Hoboken homicide detectives.

Mack Dawson was also in the group as a courtesy for his involvement.

Then the van, accompanied by two DC cruisers and an unmarked Ford Interceptor with the detectives inside, quickly rode up G Street and out of sight.

It was surreal.

I looked over at Irene.

"You OK?"

"Yeah, it's weird but good."

I agreed.

Ben Beckett, thinking that I had impregnated his wife and that I was the birth father of his son, Eddie, had meticulously planned his revenge by murdering my girlfriend Katie Kovacs.

Although all the details remain unclear, it seems that he went to Katie's Hoboken apartment on the night that I was at the Lomachenko fight at the Garden. Then he gained access somehow. Maybe by claiming that he was an old friend of someone she knew. Maybe me. Then he incapacitated Katie. Maybe with chloroform. Then he put her in her bed and injected her with an overdose of Flunitrazepam (aka Rohypnol). Then, surely wearing surgical gloves, he set the scene and typed out her supposed suicide note, implicating me.

Something like that.

Hopefully, Katie was overwhelmed quickly.

Hopefully, her terror was short.

Hopefully, she didn't suffer anything else.

After all, the real point was to punish me.

And to implicate me as well.

Which worked pretty well at first.

"Why did you think it was Ben?" she asked.

"I started thinking about it when you told me that he was suspicious that he wasn't Eddie's father."

"But I was never aware that he knew who you were, Richie. He was definitely suspicious that I'd cheated a few times, but I always denied it."

"He was much smarter than you thought."

"I guess so."

"He figured it out somehow."

"I guess so."

"Anyway, when you told me about his suspicions, it got me wondering. Then I remembered that he was a neurologist and that he had insomnia issues."

"I don't understand."

"I once had an uncle with severe sleep issues, and he went to a sleep specialist. What they call a somnologist, and a lot of somnologists are neurologists."

"But Ben wasn't."

"No, but he'd surely know about it. And he'd definitely know that a common treatment for insomnia in some countries is Rohypnol."

"Roofies? The date rape drug?"

"Exactly."

"But I thought the drug was illegal in the US?"

"It is, and in most European countries, but it's still available in many other countries. Like Mexico."

She understood.

"And I'd told you that he'd been to a medical conference in Cancun."

"Exactly. It was all circumstantial, but when I told Mack Dawson to tell all this stuff to the detectives at Hoboken Homicide, they got some detectives from down here in DC to start snooping around, and some of your husband's colleagues told them enough about Cancun for an arrest warrant. Apparently, your husband left the conference early, which has now been confirmed, then flew into Newark to do what he did to Katie. From what Mack tells me, they've already found a stash of Mexican-purchased Rohypnol at your house in Great Falls this morning after your husband left for work. My guess is that they're probably finding even more of the drug right across the street as they search his office."

There were still three DC cruisers parked in front of the building along with a forensics van.

Yesterday, the Hoboken cops had alerted Irene about what was happening, and they told her to lie low in Florida until it was over. Instead, she impulsively flew up to Dulles last night, checked into the airport Hilton, and called me.

She wanted to be there.

"I want to see the bastard get arrested."

So did I.

Now we were together on G Street.

"Do you think they'll get him for the murder?" she wondered.

"I don't know, but they've already got him for possession of an illegal drug."

"Would that put him in jail?"

"Yes, it's a three-year mandatory. Which is a start."

"Yeah, but I think they'll also get him for the murder," she decided.

"Why?"

"Because he's always the bigshot, the big mouth, and he has anger issues."

"But won't he ask for a lawyer right away?"

"Maybe, but Ben always thinks he's smarter than everybody else. I think that he'll want to talk, and if it gets heated, he might incriminate himself."

It sounded too good to be true.

"Let's hope so."

There was silence for a few moments, and she knew what was on my mind.

"Go ahead and ask me," she said in frustration.

"Fine, is the kid mine?"

"No, he's not."

"How will I ever know for sure?"

She was prepared.

"I'm planning to run a DNA test, Richie, and I'll send you a copy of the report. I want to move on with my life. No more Ben. No more you. Maybe I'll even read that book you mentioned."

Meaning the *Philothea*.

"It's done me a lot of good," I assured her, "but I'll still be checking my mail every day for the DNA report."

She shook her head in exasperation.

"You're *such* a pain in the ass, Richie! Why can't men behave themselves? I hate men!"

"Not from what I remember, Irene."

She laughed.

I drove her to the Hilton and dropped her at the entrance. Then I went over to Dulles for my flight back to Newark.

Chapter 29

Hudson County Courthouse

(Monday, 4/18/22)

He looked pretty pathetic.

Fine with me.

Cal stood facing the judge for his arraignment. His lawyer stood beside him. The place was packed, and the press was lurking both outside the courtroom and outside the four-columned Beaux-Arts Courthouse built in 1906 in Jersey City.

The room, as Mack explained earlier, was one of eight working courtrooms inside the courthouse, some of which have been used as sets for various movies and television shows, like *Law & Order*.

But this was real.

I sat in the back with Mack, and I could see Angie sitting off to the side with her lawyer and Zabrina.

Cal Calhoun only spoke once, weakly pleading "not guilty" to the several charges related to the rape that occurred ten years ago in my Hoboken condo. Despite his plea, Cal looked both guilty and broken. Maybe I should have had some compassion for the man, especially since he'd helped me early in my career, especially since I'm supposed to be a Christian, but I couldn't find much sympathy in my heart. After all, I was there in Hoboken that night. The best I could do was plan to say some prayers for his damaged soul later tonight.

Mack Dawson told me that Cal's lawyers would most probably arrange a guilty deal, given that there were two reliable witnesses. Me on the night of the rape, and Zabrina afterwards. Along with all the photos that Zabrina took. Along with the damning DNA found on Angie's panties, which Zabrina had preserved for ten long years.

As for me, I was fine with a plea deal as long as the bastard went to jail because it would spare Angie from having to relive everything on the witness stand.

Today's arraignment was over rather quickly, and Angie's protective lawyer rushed her out of the courtroom. Through the crowd. Through the phalanx of news reporters. Fortunately, no one bothered with me, as Zabrina came back to where I was sitting.

She looked a bit beaten down herself. Pretty as always, but definitely frazzled. After all, Zabrina had started the whole thing with her cavalier comments on the *Sportswomen* podcast.

She leaned over.

"She'd like to see you," she said.

"Where?"

"Her lawyer's taking her to one of the small conference rooms. B-8."

I looked over at Mack.

"Yeah, I know where it is," he assured me.

Zabrina lingered.

"I'm sorry, Richie, for the mess I've created."

She meant it.

I tried to be as good as I could be about it.

"Maybe it'll work out for the best."

"Maybe," she said thoughtfully, not fully convinced. Then she vanished into the milling crowd.

"Let's get out of here," Mack said, "before some sports nut recognizes you."

We stood up and left the courtroom, slipping past the frenetic reporters. We walked down a few empty wide corridors to room B-8. Angie's lawyer, a trim tall guy in a dark blue suit, was standing at the door. He was the kind of lawyer that inspired confidence, and Mack had assured me that he was one of the best.

"She's inside," he said unnecessarily, then opened the door for me. I went inside alone. It was a small room with wooden paneling and a big wooden table. Angie sat alone in one of the many chairs. She looked lovely, wearing a hunter green Burberry trench over a light green dress with a white lace collar.

She looked at me and smiled.

Weakly.

"A woman can change her mind, right?"

It wasn't flip.

It was both serious and pensive.

"Of course," I agreed, "but why?"

She shrugged.

"The more I thought about it, the more I wanted to see him punished."

"Sounds good to me, Angie. I've been told that he'll probably confess and cut a deal of some kind."

"Which is fine, as long as he does some time in prison."

"I was told that five years is likely."

"Yeah, I've been told the same thing."

"It's not nearly enough, Angie, but it's something. Personally, I think he should be hung in Church Square Park."

She smiled.

"Yeah, that'd be nice."

Then she stood up and looked at me intently.

"You've made things easy for me, Richie. You helped me that night, and you've supported me ever since that stupid podcast."

"I still will, Angie."

She leaned into me and kissed me on the cheek.

"Thank you," she said.

Then she smiled again.

"Now it's time to try and escape this madhouse!"

Exactly.

When she left the room, I prayed that she'd never have to return to the madhouse again.

Chapter 30

Postscript

(Thursday, 11/17/22)

"**A**ll right."

It was a simple two-word text, but it changed my life. It was Cindy's response to my question at Trout Field.

I want to try again.

And her response that day:

Let me think about it.

So she'd thought it over and was willing to give it a try. Her text came two days after the baseball game at Mike Trout Field, and we went to the Roadhouse for dinner two nights later. It was a slow start, but a good one, and we laughed a lot.

Like old times.

I was doing my best.

Over the next few months, we did a bunch of special stuff together, getting closer and closer.

Highlights included:

5/14 *South Pacific* at MPAC in Morristown. Cindy's favorite musical.

6/5 Angels at Phillies. Not Mike Trout's best night, but he did score a run, even though the Angels lost 9-7. Cindy cheered wildly for the Phillies and for all of Mike Trout's individual at-bats, which meant that she was happy. So was I. Afterwards she kissed me for the first time in twelve years. It was serious, and it was delicious, and it was marvelous.

6/12 Boxing Hall of Fame Inductions. Cindy's a sports fan in general, but always a bit uneasy about the violence of boxing, but she decided to come along anyway. We spent three days in Canastota, New York, and she had a great time. Because of Covid, the 2020 and 2021 inductions had been cancelled, so the selections for all three years were inducted on 6/12. It was an amazing list. Bernard Hopkins, Andre Ward, Wladimir Klitschko, Christy Martin, Sugar Shane Moseley, Miguel Cotto, Roy Jones Jr., Holly Holm, Kathy Duva (New Jersey's own), and many others. She especially enjoyed meeting Andre Ward and the Executioner (Bernard Hopkins).

6/28 Astros at Mets. We rooted fruitlessly against the hated Astros, who won easily 9-1. At least Pete Alonso got a hit, and Starling Marte hit a double, but most of it was totally exasperating. Yet

Cindy seemed to enjoy her exasperations, and she especially enjoyed booing the cheating Astros.

7/24 MLB Hall of Fame Inductions in Cooperstown. It was another great lineup: Jim Kaat, Minnie Minoso, Tony Oliva, Buck O'Neil who starred for the old Kansas City Monarchs of the Negro Leagues back in the late thirties and forties, and most significantly for me, Gil Hodges, one of my father's all-time favorites, who'd died back in 1972. Afterwards, we met with some of Gil's family, including his daughter who spoke beautifully at the induction ceremony. It was another fantastic weekend.

10/22 Rutgers Homecoming Game against Indiana. Which we won 24-17 led by Scarlet Knights' QB Noah Vedral.

Somewhere in the midst of all this, we fell in love again, which was very easy for me. Cindy, of course, was more wary in the beginning, but soon we were back together again. On the weekdays, she continued happily teaching Latin at Princeton Prep, and I got going on my Gil Hodges project. Then we'd spent the weekends together, often down the Shore in Sea Girt.

Cindy had come to believe that what I'd told her was true. That I'd changed. Which I believed as well. I'd read de Sales three times, and I'd done a lot of soul-searching. I've never really liked that word, but to be honest about it, it's exactly what I'd been doing. Trying to honestly evaluate my life and my behavior in light of my relationship with God.

Thus, soul-searching.

So what about sports?

What about my obsession with something so frivolous?

Like an alcoholic who has to face his problem, I did my best to face mine. Sports, as de Sales pointed out in the early seventeenth century, aren't inherently evil in themselves, what's evil is how someone like me allows a simple entertainment to take over his life and damage his faith, his marriage, and all of his relationships. So I think I've managed to finally put things in perspective.

I would be a Catholic first, a husband second, and still continue with, within limits, my vocation as a person who writes about sports. But now I'd do so with a much broader view.

With a Christian perspective.

Yes, I would still continue with my somewhat stupid yet hopefully entertaining collection of quotes to be entitled *Quips: Sports Quotes*. Which now included a selection of sports quotes related to religion.

[Which I hope the old man in the tower will appreciate.]

My faith doesn't make me perfect, it makes me forgiven. (Peyton Manning)

There's more to me than just this jersey I wear, and that's Christ living inside me. (Steph Curry)

Talent is God-given. Be humble. Fame is man-given. Be grateful. Conceit is self-given. Be careful. (John Wooden)

I definitely feel I have this amazing gift that God has blessed me with, and it's all about using it to the best of my ability. (Allyson Felix)

I give all the glory to God. It's kind of a win-win situation. The glory goes up to Him and the blessings fall down on me. (Gabby Douglas)

Everything starts with God in my career, and it will finish with God. (Mariano Rivera)

If I didn't work as hard as I could, then I think it would be a bit like saying, 'God, thanks for giving me this ability, but I don't really care about it.' (Tim Tebow)

I know that I'm on the football field to glorify Him before everything. (Patrick Mahomes)

Etc.

I'm also, as mentioned to Irene in Washington, DC, writing a book about the sports life and personal life of Gil Hodges. Naturally, I already knew a lot about Hodges since he was the man who created the 1969 Miracle Mets. He'd been hired in 1968 to manage the hapless expansion club that had suffered through six previous losing seasons all ending in tenth place in the ten-team National League, except for a nine-place finish in 1966. Yet somehow, in his second year at the helm, Hodges had the Mets winning a hundred games, followed by a sweep of the Braves in the inaugural NLCS, then, after losing the first game to the powerhouse Baltimore Orioles, the Mets won four games in a row to win the 1969 World Series.

Amazin'!

Yes, the Mets had Hall of Famer Tom Seaver, as well as some other quality players like Tommy Agee, Jerry Koosman, and Ed Kranepool, but there was no doubt that the calm confident direction of Gil Hodges had made it all possible. As outfielder Ron Swoboda once explained, "To put it simply, there would have been no 1969 World Championship for the Mets without Gil Hodges." A sentiment echoed by all of his teammates.

What I didn't know about the man was that his entire life was motivated by a deep Catholicism. By all accounts, he was a Catholic gentleman, a devoted family man, and a proud patriot. Born in Indiana, he served as a Marine anti-aircraft gunner during the battles of Tinian and Okinawa in World War II and received the Bronze Star for "heroism under fire."

In 1947, he was called up to the Brooklyn Dodgers, and he had a stellar eighteen-year career until injuries forced him into coaching. Hodges was an eight-time All-Star, drove in the only two runs in the deciding game of the 1955 World Series, and was generally considered the best fielding first baseman of his time. He hit 361 home runs, which is still second only to his teammate Duke Snider in franchise history, and he was the most popular player in Brooklyn, beloved by an especially rabid fan base. One year when he was in a bad slump, a Brooklyn priest ended Sunday Mass by encouraging his parishioners to "go home and say a prayer for Gil Hodges."

At the end of his career, Hodges ended up on the Mets in their very first season in 1962, and, rather ironically, he hit the first home run in Mets history. Eventually he managed the Washington Senators for a few years before coming back to the Mets as manager in 1968. He was renowned as a man of remarkable integrity and kindness, who was also witty with a dry sense of humor.

As teammate Duke Snider once put it:

Gil was a great player, but an even greater man.

In 1947 when Hodges was called up to the Dodgers, it was the same year that Jackie Robinson joined the team and broke baseball's color line. Gil and Jackie immediately became close friends both on and off the field, often spending time with their wives at each other's homes. Gil was always supportive of his friend and teammate, and after Gil's funeral in 1972 (after Gil's deadly heart attack), Jackie told Gil's son, "Next to my son's death, this is the worst day of my life."

Sadly, Jackie Robinson died six months later.

So Hodges was exactly the kind of man that I was eager to write about. An inspiring man, admired by everyone, who excelled at sports but never let it take over his life.

So how was Richard Ramsey doing?

How was he doing with his attempts to keep sports at bay in his life?

You decide.

Here's how I've rearranged my life.

Three days each week are absolute cold turkey from sports, with the weekends reserved for whatever Cindy wants to do. Sometimes, at *her* discretion, that might include sports, like occasional Phillies games or a Mets game.

Somehow, I've managed to finagle my way into a Jets Catholic prayer group every Wednesday night up in the Meadowlands with various players and staff. Which has done me a lot of good. I also volunteer for two hours every Sunday after Mass at St. Ladislaus doing odd jobs for Fr. Nagy. I'm also, to broaden my horizons, reading a new book every week from a list that I've requested from Cindy. Since I enjoyed *Moby-Dick* so much, her list includes, along with selected devotional works and hagiographies, a lot of fiction (dramas and novels), beginning with Sophocles (who's a real mind-bender) and Aeschylus.

"We'll gradually work you up to Vergil," she explained, sounding very much like a devoted Latinist.

"What about Shakespeare?" I wondered.

"Slow your roll, junior! You're nowhere ready yet!"

Fine, so I've got Vergil and Dante and some others to wade through first before tackling the English guy.

All of which I'm greatly enjoying despite my endless embarrassment at being so uneducated.

So stupid.

Anyway, that gives you the idea. It's certainly not the life of a saint, but it's far better than the monomaniacal rut that I've been trapped in for decades.

I'm trying, dear Lord!

Praise the Lord!

Yesterday, all my trying paid off.

Cindy and I were remarried in the eyes of the law at the County Clerk's office on Bayard Street in New Brunswick. It was low-key but joyous occasion, witnessed by her sister Melanie (who's apparently willing to give me "another chance") and my cousin Rebeka.

It was one of the best days of my life.

November 16.

The feast of St. Margaret of Scotland.

Exactly twelve years after our *real* marriage in the eyes of God.

In case you're wondering, old man, assuming that you might ever wonder about such things, Cindy and I reconsummated our marriage back in July in Cooperstown, New York, during the MLB Hall of Fame weekend. Despite our separation of twelve years and all my multifarious misbehaviors, we were still man and wife, and I certainly don't have to remind you about Catholic marital theology!

Now we're now planning a second honeymoon in the Scottish Highlands.

"I won't even think about sports," I promised her.

"Well then, I guess I'll have to attend the Highland Games alone!"

Which sure sounds like a lot of fun to me.

Whatever Cindy wants.

Oh, yeah, one more thing.

Two nights ago I met with Katie's cousin Lili on the Rutgers Mall near Willie the Silent.

She was pleasant as always, and she gave me a warm hug, but she was confused about why I wanted to meet.

"What's up, Richie?"

I handed her a wallet.

A man's leather wallet.

"What's this?"

"Did you know, Lili?"

"Know what?"

She was genuinely confused.

"That it was Katie's cousins who beat the crap out of me."

Meaning Bryan Sykes and his brother Colin Sykes.

Lili was shocked.

"Of course not, Richie!"

Then she remembered.

"New Year's Day?"

"Yes, they pretended to be muggers, and they tried to get my wallet. They were hoping to make it look more believable as a random mugging, as they kicked and pounded me to the ground, but I got a hold of Bryan's wallet instead. He didn't even realize it at the time, and then a car's headlights approached in our direction, and they got scared and ran off."

"If you knew it was Bryan and Colin, why didn't you tell the police?"

"Should I have?"

"Of course, Richie! I saw your face back then. You were a mess. Why didn't you say anything?"

I told her the truth.

"I felt that I deserved it."

"What! Why?"

I shrugged.

"I believed that Katie's death had something to do with me. Which turned out to be true."

Lili knew, of course, about the arrest of Irene's husband Ben Beckett eight months ago, and she also knew that, as Irene had predicted, Beckett had foolishly incriminated himself and eventually confessed to the murder.

"But it wasn't your fault, Richie," Lili insisted.

"If I hadn't got involved with Irene Beckett, nothing would have ever happened to Katie."

Which was undeniable.

She thought it over.

"Didn't Irene Beckett happen before you met Katie?"

"Yes."

She looked at me intently.

"Did you ever cheat on Katie?"

"Never."

Then she wondered about something else.

"Did you ever cheat on Cindy?"

"Never."

"Well, I think you're being too hard on yourself, Richie."

"I'm good at that."

"Katie would forgive you. I'm sure of it."

"I hope so. I need all the forgiveness I can get.

"It seems that Cindy has forgiven you."

"Yes, I've been blessed with that."

Then we talked about my remarriage, then we wished each other well. Afterward, I went over to St. Ladislaus Church and lit some candles for Katie, for Lili, for Cindy, for everyone.

Even the blind old man in the tower.

"*Gloria in excelsis Deo!*"

III.

2023

Addendum:

[This addendum has been written at the request of Fr. John C. Colt. Requested as follows:

Three evenings ago, Cindy was at home in our cottage at Sea Girt. There was a knock on the front door.

Unfortunately, I was off in the Meadowlands.

She opened the door.

"He was the scariest-looking person I've ever seen," she told me later, "but somehow, despite his natural intimidation, I didn't feel threatened at all. Probably because I knew who he was from all the news reports over the years."

He was oddly polite.

"My name is John Colt, and I'd like a moment with Mr. Ramsey."

He was, as Cindy has described, tall and solid and rugged, maybe two inches over six foot, maybe late thirties. He wore a dark designer suit (Armani?), a navy button-down dress shirt, a thin black tie, and black leather shoes. He wore dark shades, was not unattractive despite the fact that his dark black hair was greased straight back, and he had a small scar in the shape of a cross in the center of his forehead. From Cindy's point of view, he looked like some kind of mob enforcer, and she believed that he was wearing a shoulder holster.

Yet she still wasn't afraid of him, despite his habit of staring right through her through his dark shades.

She told him the truth.

"My husband's out for the evening."

He thought it over.

"Could you give him a message?"

"Of course."

"Tell him my uncle would like an addendum. A brief account of the final outs of the WBC."

Which seemed so ridiculous that Cindy was tempted to laugh, but she didn't.

The man was dead serious.

"I'll let him know."

He nodded, then added:

"Brief."

"Yes, I'll tell him."

Then he walked away, got into his black Lincoln, and drove off into the New Jersey falling darkness.

Cindy swears that she could hear Springsteen fading away into the night.

"Dancing in the Dark."

John Colt is the most famous private detective in the Metro area, maybe in the country, and I was sorry that I missed him. It was Colt's rude secretary, of course, who'd recommended Mack Dawson years ago, for whom I'm ever grateful.

But let's face it, who wouldn't want to meet John Colt? At least I was able to enjoy Cindy's eager recounting of her own peculiar encounter. We both wondered, of course, why he felt the need to come down to the Shore in person, and we have no idea. Cindy suggested that maybe he'd been reading (out loud) my completed thirty-chapter memoir for Fr. Colt, and maybe he was curious to get a look at the guy who wrote it.

"Through his dark black shades!" she kidded.

Maybe.

Who knows?

Regardless, here's the requested brief addendum.]

(Tuesday, 3/21/23)

Would it happen?

Was it possible that the two greatest baseball players in the world (who were MLB teammates) would face each other in the final championship game of the World Baseball Classic?

Not very likely right?

I was sitting in jam-packed LoanDepot Park in Miami. I wasn't down here on any kind of assignment. I was just there to enjoy the game and for another more personal reason.

My wife Cindy was with me.

She was the one who'd suggested the idea.

"Let's go see Mike," she said.

So we did.

Japan vs. the United States.

With Mike Trout serving as the captain of the US team.

At the top of the ninth inning, as everyone was hoping, Shohei Ohtani was brought in as a reliever to save the game for Japan. The score was Japan 3 and the US 2. The first batter was Jeff McNeil who walked, but Mookie Betts then hit into a double-play. Two outs.

Guess who was up next?

Ohtani's teammate on the California Angels, Mike Trout, who'd won the MVP three times and came in second four times, who was generally considered the greatest player alive (and one of the best of all-time) until hit-and-pitch Ohtani joined the team in 2017.

Now they were considered the two best in the world, and they were facing each other for the World Baseball Championship.

A sportswriter's dream.

A sports fan's dream.

The first pitch was a breaking ball that missed.

0-1.

The next pitch was a 100-mile fastball that blew by Trout.

1-1.

The next fastball missed the strike zone.

2-1.

Another 100-mile fastball blew by Trout, which doesn't happen that often.

2-2.

Another fastball missed.

3-2.

Full count.

Trout, with a home run, could tie the game. With a hit or a walk, he could keep US hopes alive.

I couldn't believe what I was seeing.

No one could.

Except maybe Cindy, who was standing and cheering like a crazy person.

Ohtani wound up and unexpectedly threw a slider that Trout swung at and missed.

Amazing!

The Japanese players swarmed the mound and Ohtani as the World Champions.

Cindy sat down in her seat next to me.

Later that night, I read that some guy pointed out that Trout seldom ever struck out with three missed swings. Only twenty-four times in his previous 6,174 MLB plate appearances.

0.38%

The crowd was stunned.

So was I, but Cindy, who'd followed Mike's career ever since he was a little kid in Millville, seemed to take it in stride.

"Oh, well, even Mike can't get a hit every time."

Which was true.

"What did Babe Ruth say?" she asked. "About striking out?"

I cited the famous quote:

Every strike brings me closer to the next home run.

Yeah, Ruth said "strike" not "strikeout," but it's the same thing.

"He'll be fine," she decided, then she looked at me directly.

"Guess what, love?" she said.

I had no idea what was happening.

"What?"

"I'm pregnant."

After the jolt passed through my brain, I kissed her on the mouth. I can't ever remember being so happy, which is why, I guess, that the old priest in the tower wanted me to write this little coda.

Richard Ramsey III was born eight months later in St. Peter's Hospital in New Brunswick, New Jersey, to the most wonderful woman in the world and her ever-trying husband, a sportswriter among other much more important things.

The end.

[God bless you, Fr. Colt!]

S.D.G.

About the author

William Baer, author of over forty books, has been the recipient of a Guggenheim Fellowship, a Fulbright (Portugal), a fellowship in fiction from the National Endowment for the Arts, the T.S. Eliot Award, and the Jack Nicholson Screenwriting Award. His various books include *Times Square and Other Stories*; *Advocatus Diaboli*; *Psalter: A Sequence of Catholic Sonnets*; *The Heretic*; *The Dark Knight of Assisi*; *The Gravedigger*; *Classic American Films*; *Luís de Camões: Selected Sonnets* (translations from the Portuguese); the Jack Colt mystery series (*New Jersey Noir*); and the Deirdre mystery series. He is a graduate of Rutgers, NYU, South Carolina, the Johns Hopkins Writing Seminars, and USC Cinema. He was also the founding editor of *The Formalist*, the director of the St. Robert Southwell Summer Workshops, and the film critic and poetry editor at *Crisis*.

His other writings have appeared in a wide range of literary, religious, and/or cultural journals including *The American Scholar, Chronicles, First Things, The Hudson Review, The Kenyon Review, London Magazine, Modern Age, National Review, The New Criterion, Ploughshares, Poetry, Quadrant, The Southern Review, The University B ookman, The Virginia Quarterly Review,* and *The Wanderer*.

He lives happily in a log cabin in northern New Jersey and loves pizza, books, sports, and chocolate.

272

Also by the author

Catholic-Themed Novels by William Baer:

Advocatus Diaboli

The Heretic

Jacinta

The Dark Knight of Assisi

Selected Other Novels:

New Jersey Noir

New Jersey Noir: Cape May

New Jersey Noir: Barnegat Light

The Gravedigger

Novel

Murder in Times Square

Murder in Nashville

Annie Oakley Mystery

Mary Pickford Mystery

Central Park

Companion

The Sweet Science

Equinox

WILLIAM BAER

Selected Other Books:

Times Square and Other Stories

One-And-Twenty Tales

Psalter: A Sequence of Catholic Sonnets

Formal Salutations: New & Selected Poems

Classic American Films: Conversations with the Screenwriters

Elia Kazan: Interviews

Luís de Camões: Selected Sonnets (translations)

Writing Metrical Poetry

Conversations with Derek Walcott